Christine Pullein-Thompson has been involved with horses all her life—she opened a riding school with her sisters when she was fourteen. She started writing at fifteen and published her first book with her sisters Diana and Josephine. Christine has written more than 90 books which have been translated into nine languages. She is best known for her pony books but has also written the highly successful Jessie series about a dog and general fiction stories for younger readers.

Christine has four children and lives with her husband Julian Popescu in a moated Parsonage in Suffolk with two horses, a dog and a cat.

Other Pony Books by Christine Pullein-Thompson

Published by *Cavalier Paperbacks*

Stolen Ponies
I Rode A Winner
The Lost Pony
A Pony In Distress

FOR WANT OF A SADDLE

Christine Pullein-Thompson

**CAVALIER
PAPERBACKS**

© Christine Pullein-Thompson 1994

Published by Cavalier Paperbacks 1994
PO Box 1821, Warminster, Wilts BA12 0YD

Cover Design by Michelle Bellfield
Cover Photograph by Alistair Fyfe
Courtesy of The Infantry Saddle Club, Warminster

ISBN 1–899470–04–2

Typeset in New Century Schoolbook and Ottawa
by Ann Buchan (Typesetters), Shepperton
Printed and bound by
Cox and Wyman, Reading, Berkshire

CONTENTS

1. He Hates Us   7

2. Mr Stone   16

3. The Girl   24

4. Let's Make A Bargain   33

5. Learning to Ride   41

6. You Won't See Me Any More   49

7. Driving Tomtit   57

8. David Comes   64

9. What Are You Dreaming About?   74

10. The Riding School   82

11. Gymkhana Entries   90

12. Produce Stall   99

13. We Couldn't Go On   109

14. The Saddle   119

Chapter One

HE HATES US

The garden was walled; their house was set in that same wall; it also faced the winding country road. It was a small, neat, mellow, red-brick cottage, with gables and bright green window-frames. The Smallbones watched the removal van disappearing along the country road.

"It's quiet here all right," exclaimed Mrs Smallbone, standing small and out of place in a black coat and town shoes. Mr Smallbone held the twins, Rachel and Kelly.

Katie, who was small with short brown hair and nearly ten, said "Where's the pony? David said there was a pony we could ride."

Nothing was as she had expected it to be. She had expected a large, rambling market garden, divided from a paddock by a wire fence, and in that paddock she had imagined a pony—the pony David Smith had said Mr Stone was anxious for them to ride. But the garden had been a garden for years, and had straight, neat paths and fruit trees trained to climb walls, and there was no pony to be seen anywhere. It seemed to Katie that she was to be disappointed as she had been so often before. Nothing ever comes right for us, she thought, staring at a cluster of snowdrops without seeing them. One might as well give up hoping ... If one doesn't hope one can't be disappointed, that stands to reason.

Mick being optimistic by nature, stood thinking, the pony must be somewhere; the countryside is marvellous. Look at those primroses! And we're going to be all together at last. The twins will have the whole garden to play in. He wanted to break into song, to cheer wildly, to run down the road to a telephone box and ring up David Smith and cry into the mouthpiece, "Thank you for everything. Thank you." We owe all this to David, thought Mick, looking at the cottage with its newly painted window-frames, so different from the room and kitchenette in the large industrial town where they had lived for so long.

"There's room for some chickens at the back," said Mr Smallbone, turning towards the cottage.

There was a large notice by the gate which read Hillsborough Market Garden, and a blackboard which announced Cut Flowers, Rhubarb, Brussels Sprouts. It was March and already the very air smelt of spring. Birds were singing in the trees, hens cackled in the distance; in the garden were snowdrops and in sunny corners violets raised small faces to the sun. And on the nut trees there were lambs' tails.

The Smallbones ate a picnic lunch sitting on suitcases; the twins were put to bed. Mick and Katie washed up in the kitchen.

"Yes, and two gardens—ours and the market one."

They gazed at one another. Katie had a small face with brown eyes. She hadn't Mick's determination;

impulsive and generous, she often felt defeated in the face of disaster. She was restless now, and the rustling, whispering March wind outside seemed to match her mood. She wanted to be riding along a country road wearing the right clothes, sitting properly, holding her reins elegantly with an air of detachment, as though she spent her life riding. But even if there is a pony, we haven't any clothes—not proper ones, only jeans and trainers; and we can't ride, she thought, throwing down the dishcloth. Some people have all the luck—clothes, ponies, riding lessons.

Mick was different. He only wanted to ride, to see a pony's ears in front of him, to smell the smell of horse again. The rest was a challenge. We'll get clothes somehow, he thought, looking at his own faded jeans. We'll ride Mr Stone's pony in shows. We'll learn to jump. I'll pass the eleven-plus and become a vet. I shall specialise in horses. I'll own a Boxer dog and a red car. He had a short, straight nose which he wrinkled, a small mouth which turned up at the corners. He's game, people said.

More than anything at this moment, he wanted to see the pony. They had found one once, a lovely chestnut, a stray they thought, which was theirs to ride. But all too soon they had found he belonged to a film star's daughter; and now that short episode, which had meant so much at the time, seemed more like a dream. But out of that dream had come the market garden their father was to run, the little mellow house, which smelt of the country, of sun and flowers, wind and rain; and most of all, the pony they hadn't seen.

"He's just an old pony with creaking joints," David had said, Mick remembered.

All that had happened in the autumn; now spring had come and here they were in the country at last, with the buds appearing in the hedges, and the grass turning green, and everything seeming to whisper of the sunlit days ahead.

"Mum's sitting down. Let's see if we can find the pony," Mick suggested, hanging his tea towel on a convenient nail. Their father had gone to see Mr Stone. The two children walked down one of the neat paths. They saw now that there were weeds on the borders; an old fork, plunged deep into the brown earth, stood among a row of tattered Brussels sprouts; a glass frame lay broken by a greenhouse. They found a gate in a wall. It gave access to a drive, bordered with yews.

"We mustn't get lost. Really we mustn't. The twins will wake up soon. We can't leave Mum to do everything," Katie replied.

"We're only going to be a moment. We must see the pony, mustn't we?" Mick replied.

"Where's Mr Stone's house? He was building himself a bungalow, wasn't he?"

"Yes, because of his heart. He can only do the accounts now, and the ordering. We're to do the rest."

Mick wondered for a moment whether his father knew enough. He had grown up in the country. But did he understand the trees which grew up the wall in the garden? Did he understand flowers? Supposing we don't know enough? Supposing we fail?

thought Mick suddenly. How can we go back after tasting this? The twins will pine for the garden.

"Look! There he is. Really he is!" cried Katie. On the other side of the railings a bay pony cropped sparse grass. He had large ears, a small eye. His long back was hollow, his muzzle grey. His neck was thin, his shoulder straight. They stood and stared. "He isn't like Blue Grass. But David said he wouldn't be like that. He said—what did he say?" asked Mick.

"That he had pulled a roller on a cricket pitch, that now he didn't do much," replied Katie.

"Come on, pony," said Mick climbing the rails. The pony raised his ugly head, put back his ears. For a second he seemed to sneer before he walked away.

"I wish it was Prince . . ."

"Don't be ridiculous," cried Mick. "This pony's just right to learn on. David said so, didn't he? We're jolly lucky."

"Don't pretend. You're disappointed too. I can hear it in your voice," Katie said.

"I'm not. I tell you we're lucky. What is the saying? You know, Handsome is as handsome does."

"But we can see what he does. He hates us."

"You always expect too much, Katie. You always have; then you're disappointed. I'm different. I say one should make the best of what one has."

They called the pony again, and walked towards him. It seemed that he could feel them approaching without having to turn round; at any rate each time they drew near, his ears flashed back, his untidy tail swished and he moved away.

"We'd better go back now. We can't leave Mum to

do everything," Katie said. She could see the future now, the pony they couldn't catch standing in his paddock like a monument to their failure.

"We only need a bucket of oats. He'll come then, you'll see," replied Mick, climbing the railing after his sister. "His halter must be somewhere, and a set of harness."

"But no saddle," said Katie, opening the gate into the garden.

"We can borrow one."

"Who from?"

"David."

The twins were crying when they reached the house.

"I thought you were never coming. Here are their coats. Take them out for a bit in the pram, Katie. Poor little souls, everything's strange," said Mrs Smallbone.

"Where's the pram?"

"In the shed."

"We found the pony," Mick said. "He's a bay, about thirteen hands, just right to learn on."

"Are you happy now then?" asked Mrs Smallbone, pushing Rachel into a pair of leggings.

"Yes. Is Dad still with Mr Stone? I hope he asks about the pony. We can't find a halter or anything."

"Give him time," said Mrs Smallbone.

Mick didn't want to give anyone time. He wanted to be riding along the country roads. He had to remind himself that the whole Easter holidays lay ahead. By May, he thought, he and Katie should be able to trot and canter without holding on to the saddle, which, of course, brought him back to their biggest problem—the saddle.

His father came in then, tall, broad-shouldered, he had Mick's mouth and eyes.

"Well, how was the gentleman?" asked Mrs Smallbone.

"Mr Stone? Fair. He's a nice old man," replied Mr Smallbone. "Where are the twins? We'd better get the house straight."

"What about the pony? What did he say about that?" asked Mick.

"What pony?"

"The pony we were to ride," Mick's dreams seemed to be disintegrating into dust before his eyes. "The pony. You must remember," he said, staring into his father's face.

"Perhaps he's changed his mind. We'll have to wait and see. We can't ask for favours. Come on, Mum. Let's get the place straight. Make it look a bit like home." He picked up a chair and disappeared whistling, while Mick stood small and stunned, until his determination came back, and with it hope and resolution.

Meanwhile, Katie pushed Kelly and Rachel in the large, old-fashioned pram past fields and cottages, and imagined herself driving the bay pony instead, her mother holding the twins. The sun came out, dazzling bright after weeks of fog and rain and her heart rose with it until she saw herself and Mick galloping across green fields, teaching the twins to ride, grooming the bay pony till his coat shone bright and reddish brown like polished mahogany. There

13

will be no dirty smoke to blacken Mum's washing and to spoil the windows when they've just been cleaned. And Dad's overalls will be covered with mud instead of oil, and perhaps later we'll be able to have a washing machine, she thought, and for a moment everything seemed perfect, as thought everything she had ever wanted was coming true.

Then she remembered that the bay was ugly and cross, that they hadn't a saddle. The twins started to cry and the sun went in. Her legs started to ache and she turned for home. Probably David was wrong, probably the bay isn't even broken for riding, thought Katie, pushing the large untidy pram. We aren't likely to find another lost pony. It'll be like all my other dreams. The twins, sensing her mood, started to cry louder than ever; an angry March wind whipped her face, and thin rain began to fall. Nothing comes right for us, she thought, starting to run. We never have any luck, at least only once and that seems years ago now.

Rachel was calling, "Mum, Mum, Mum!" now, until her voice gradually rose to a scream. The rain fell faster. Katie reached the house.

"What news?" cried Katie, carrying the twins into the kitchen, where Mick was laying the table for tea.

"Dad didn't even ask. Never mentioned the pony. We'll have to see Mr Stone, that's all, Katie," he said.

"Yes, tomorrow. and we must remember to wash our faces and comb our hair; but I don't suppose it'll come to anything. David must have made a mistake. After all, he's human," Katie said. Her face was suddenly shut and bitter.

"No, he wouldn't have made a mistake like that. He would have realised how much we cared before he even asked. We'll see Mr Stone tomorrow."

"Whatever shall we say?"

"Please sir, may we ride your pony?"

"That won't be enough, replied Katie, removing the twins' coats. We must say that perhaps we made a mistake, but . . ."

"And we must ask about the saddle and bridle."

"Yes; though I don't suppose it'll come to anything. We never have any luck. How do you know we'll ever be able to catch the pony?"

"We can always drive him into a corner."

"And get kicked."

"He's not as bad as that."

"How do you know?"

"I just do."

Their mother came in then. "Where's tea, Mick?" she cried. "You haven't even put the kettle on."

"We were talking about the pony."

"That won't get tea," she said.

Chapter Two

MR STONE

They stood knocking on the bungalow door. It was a very new bungalow with large windows which seemed to glare, and the same green paint on the door as brightened the window-frames of their house. Someone had started to build a rockery, and there was a long-haired cat washing himself by the back door.

I hate knocking on doors, thought Katie. It makes me feel like a beggar, and in a sense we are begging: Please sir, can we ride your pony? Isn't that begging?

The wind was still there, but yesterday's rain had gone in the night and already the ground was dry again.

An old man opened the door. He was wearing bedroom slippers, pyjamas, a faded blue dressing-gown.

"We've come too early. We've got him out of bed," thought Katie; but Mick was already talking.

"We're the Smallbones," he announced firmly. "I'm afraid we're rather early, sir."

The old man looked them up and down. "You'd better come in," he said.

They followed him into a small sitting room with a tiled fireplace, two armchairs and a sofa. Over the mantelpiece hung a wedding photograph, faded and stained with age.

"What can I do for you?" asked the old man.

Mick didn't know how to begin. He wished now that they had waited. He looked at Katie, but she had rolled her handkerchief into a small ball and was staring out of the window as though everything they had ever wanted was growing in Mr Stone's half-made rockery.

"It's about the pony," began Mick at last. "David Smith said we could ride him, that you said so."

"You see, we are very fond of horses," added Katie.

"What, old Nobby? He's an artful old beggar. A girl used to come and ride him, but then she couldn't catch him. I don't think she comes any more. Do you think you'll catch him?"

"Oh yes, I'm sure we can," replied Mick firmly.

"But we really need some oats and a halter," said Katie.

"There's a halter and a set of harness somewhere. Try the greenhouses," said Mr Stone, beginning to walk to the front door. "You're welcome to Nobby. It'll do him good to have some exercise."

"What about the oats?" persisted Katie.

"I've no oats. I'm afraid. Try an apple or carrot," suggested Mr Stone, holding the front door open for them.

Mick wanted to stay and ask a great many questions. But there was no chance. The front door shut behind them and they were outside again looking at the rockery and at the cat which still sat by the back door washing his paws.

"We never asked about the saddle," wailed Katie.

"I know. How could we? We'll have to manage without, that's all."

"It'll make everything twice as difficult,"

"That can't be helped."

"I don't like Nobby much as a name."

"Nor do I, because there are lots of Nobbys."

They shut the garden gate.

"Well, at least we know now that we can ride him," said Mick.

"If we can catch him."

"Let's see if we can find the halter."

"Mum said we weren't to be long. She wants us to take Rachel and Kelly to the village shop in the pram."

The wind slammed the door after them as they entered the walled garden.

"Which greenhouse shall we try first?" asked Mick.

They found the halter at last among a pile of old flower-pots, and later they found a set of harness hanging from a hook above a line of forks.

"At least there's a bridle," said Mick.

"It's all green, and the bridle's got blinkers," complained Katie.

"Perhaps we can take them off," suggested Mick.

"I suppose the girl had her own tack," said Katie, and she imagined a neatly-dressed figure in jodhpurs with fair curls protruding from under her skull-cap.

"I expect so."

"Supposing she comes again?"

"Well, he's our pony now," announced Mick firmly.

The sun was shining now, though the sky was full of small, cheerful clouds which looked as though they were playing 'catch me if you can,' or were dancing, Mick thought.

They took the harness and the halter out of the greenhouse; then they heard their mother calling: "Mick, Katie. Where are you? Mick, Katie . . ."

"We'd better go," Mick said.

"Coming," called Katie.

They picked up the dirty, green harness. Mick wound the halter round his neck. The wind blew their hair. It's always something, thought Mick. Either we're to take out the twins, or fetch the washing off the line, or lay tea. If only we could have a whole day just to ourselves.

Mrs Smallbone looked at the harness with dislike.

"I don't want that lot in my nice, tidy kitchen. You'd better put it in the back of the shed. Who said you could have it?"

"Mr Stone," answered Katie.

"You haven't been bothering him already?"

"Yes, we have."

"What do you think your father will say?"

"Well, he wouldn't ask him," Mick answered, thinking, you have to fight for everything you want in this life—at least Katie and I do.

In the afternoon they were free at last to go to the paddock again. Nobby grazed under a clump of budding chestnut trees.

Secretly they had both hoped he would seem better-looking on this second visit; his ears seemed to have grown longer, his expression more disagreeable. He looks like a very cross old man, thought Katie, the kind which snaps at you if you run your fingers along their split oak fence, or throw a ball in their garden by mistake. I'm sure he bites and kicks, and if one of us gets a leg broken, Mum will never let us ride again."

"Shall we try and drive him?" asked Mick, determined to fight to the bitter end for his dreams.

"All right. But don't get kicked."

"You are nervy," Mick said.

The pony wouldn't drive until they fetched sticks from under the chestnut tree, and by that time half the afternoon had gone. They cornered him at last, but each time they approached he turned his quarters towards them; then, quite suddenly he gave in. His ears went forward, he stretched his thin neck and took the apple Katie offered. They could have cheered then, even though the day was almost done. Another moment and Nobby was haltered.

They stared at one another.

"You see," said Mick "I knew we would succeed in the end."

They fed the pony a carrot.

"We won't ride today—it's late, and it'll make him easier to catch tomorrow," Mick said, though he was longing to climb on the pony's hollow back.

"If only we had a saddle," moaned Katie.

"There are so many if onlys. . . ."

They gave Nobby another carrot before they turned him loose, and now he wouldn't leave them; as they crossed the paddock he followed, sniffing at their pockets.

"If we halter him several times a day and don't ride him, he will soon be okay to catch. It's that wretched girl's fault. I bet she came only when she wanted to ride for the rest of the day, and, of course, he got wise to it," Mick said.

"Of course," repeated Katie.

They were jubilant now. They rushed into the kitchen crying, "We caught Nobby, and he seems to like us."

"That girl spoilt him," Mick said.

"Really she did," agreed Katie.

Their father had just come in. He stood washing dirt off his hands at the sink. Somehow even from his back they knew he was disconsolate.

"It's such a big place. Half the machinery's rusted, and you should see the raspberries—properly gone to pieces they have. Doesn't look as though they've been cared for in years. I don't know how I shall get it all straight; one pair of hands isn't enough, not for a garden that size. And I can't afford to run the van, which Mr Stone used for delivering vegetables, so we'll have to start by using the pony and cart."

Mick imagined everything over, going back to one or two rooms in an industrial town, he and Katie farmed out with foster parents again. His legs felt weak at the knees. He thought, you never know what they may do. He saw the countryside in spring and summer, the house full of flowers, the twins learning to talk, his mother sitting in the garden in a chair. It was almost all he had ever wanted in life, just this, and his chance later to be a vet.

"And if we make anything this year I'll be surprised. Half the profit sounded all right at the time, but looks different now," said Mr Smallbone, sitting down to the crowded tea table.

"Time will show, Bill," said Mrs Smallbone.

Katie suddenly didn't want any tea. Outside dusk had come gently as it does in the country, not as Katie had seen it so often, thick and dark with smoke, noisy with the roar and whistle of trains, preceded, as afternoon turned into evening, by the drone of rush-hour traffic. Katie's bedroom upstairs was the sort she had always dreamed about—small windowed, lit by the morning sun, most of all her own domain. Listening to her father's grumbling, it seemed as though a tornado had struck her thoughts.

But Mick was talking now. "Dad, Katie and I will help. Couldn't we have the hens to look after and perhaps some pigs later on? The prices are very good just now. New-laid, free range eggs are selling at £1.80 a dozen, at least, large ones are."

"We could help with the digging too. I'm very strong," said Katie, showing her thin white arms.

There was a silence, while the alarm clock ticked maddeningly, and Mick saw pigs growing large in the old empty sty he had discovered at the bottom of the garden.

It was the sort of life he had always wanted, pigs and poultry, mud and the feel of a farmyard. "It would help me to be a vet," he added.

"That's a long way off. You haven't got your eleven-plus yet," his father said. "Oh well, we'll give it a

22

trial. Maybe the strawberries will turn out better than the raspberries. Where's that book on gardening, Mum?"

Mick resolved to get up early and spend the morning putting the pigsty to rights.

Katie started to clear the table. Far away a cow was lowing; outside it was dark. Mrs Smallbone drew the curtains.

"Maybe we won't be here next winter after all, then?" she said.

Chapter Three

THE GIRL

The next day they caught Nobby and rode him in his bridle with blinkers which they had washed and polished. Mick mounted first off the railings. He pressed his heels again Nobby's bay sides and said, "Come on, walk." There didn't seem very much between his legs. He's very thin, he thought, but the summer grass will be here soon. And he saw the pony fat and round, with shining eyes and pricked ears.

"Make him move. Hurry up," cried Katie, who felt that time was running out, that any moment they might be leaving the country for ever.

"He doesn't want to go," Mick said, kicking the pony with his heels.

In the end Katie led Nobby backwards and forwards across the field until Mick said: "I'll get off. It's your turn now."

"We don't know how to ride. That's the trouble."

"I bet the girl can make him go."

"I wonder what her name is?"

The day grew warm. They took off their jerseys. Mick mounted again. "Pick me a stick, Katie," he said.

"You're not going to hit him?"

"Yes, I am."

"That's cruel," cried Katie.

"Do you want to ride? Can't you see he's obstinate? We can't give in," Mick said, dismounting and going to the chestnut trees, the pony dragging behind.

He found a stick, mounted off a mound.

"Come on, walk," he cried, raising the stick. He hit Nobby and almost simultaneously flew through the air, felt the ground rising to smack him and at the same moment saw the pony trotting away.

"Mick, are you all right?" cried Katie.

He stood up, hating the bay pony, "Can't you catch him? Why didn't you catch him?" he cried.

"I was looking at you. I was afraid you were hurt," Katie said.

They heard their mother calling, "Dinner. Mick, Katie. Where are you?"

"You'd better go," Mick said.

"We can't leave the pony with his bridle on."

"That's what I mean."

"I'm staying, too."

Hours seemed to pass before they caught the pony. They took off the bridle, looked at the broken reins.

"It doesn't matter. They were far too long," Katie said.

"They were driving reins," explained Mick.

"I think he's horrible," Katie said.

"We don't know how to ride. That's the trouble," Mick said.

They hurried back to their house, where their lunch was waiting on top of the cooker. Their mother and the twins were out. The alarm clock ticking on the windowsill said three o'clock.

"I'm not going to give up," announced Mick, eating meat and mashed potato.

"You always say that," Katie answered. "We haven't helped Dad today at all."

"There'll be time tomorrow."

"And you've torn your shorts. Did you know that?"

"No."

He sat eating, hating the whole world. I knew we were hoping for too much, Katie thought. I wish I was grown-up, working; then perhaps I should stop hoping for things. Supposing Mick doesn't get to the Grammar School. He'll never be a vet, then. He's always so cocksure, is Mick."

"I'm going back now," Mick said, taking his plate to the sink. "I'm going to make Nobby do as I say."

"You're mad. Probably no-one can ride him."

"What about the girl."

"Perhaps she can't make him go either."

"There's no point in arguing," decided Katie, looking at her brother. "But we should be helping Dad, or sweeping up the kitchen."

"You needn't come," Mick said over his shoulder.

"I'm coming. He's mine too," Katie answered.

The clock said twenty past three when they left the kitchen, and already the day was cooling. "I wish Dad would buy some chickens. I like collecting eggs," Katie said.

"Eggs won't catch Nobby," Mick replied, beginning to run.

"You mustn't keep falling off. Supposing you hurt yourself—break a leg?" Katie answered.

"I won't." He was feeling excited now, ready for

battle. I shall make him go, even if we have to stay there all night, he thought. "One has to fight. If you fail the first time, try, try again. Who said that? It's true anyway."

I don't mind falling off, he decided, opening the greenhouse door. They knotted the broken reins as they ran towards the paddock.

"I'll make him go this time, you'll see," he boasted.

"It's my turn. The first turn's mine," Katie said.

"I shall find a better stick."

"But it's my turn."

They reached the paddock railings. "Where is he?" cried Mick.

"Look over there," replied Katie.

They stood and stared.

"Are you sure?"

They couldn't believe what they saw—a bay pony cantering circles, ridden by a neat figure in check hacking jacket, jodhpurs, with dark hair under a velvet skull-cap.

"She's got a saddle," said Katie at last.

Mick felt limp. He could only think, he isn't ours to ride at all. We can't ride him, anyway. We're hopeless. We'll never learn. He was full of envy and hate as he stared at the pony and girl. She's got a saddle and bridle, he thought. It isn't fair.

Katie stood wondering, what's she called? Where does she live? Why hasn't she a pony of her own? Why does she have to steal our only hope? David Smith said ages ago that we could ride Mr Stone's pony. What did he say? But she couldn't remember. Suddenly she was fighting back tears, which came at last, thick and fast like falling rain.

"I hate her," Mick said.

"Don't. That's wicked," Katie replied.

"She can ride all right."

"She's got a saddle," Katie repeated.

"And a bridle."

Suddenly those two things were all they wanted— a saddle and bridle. We could ride then, thought Mick. I wouldn't fall off if I had stirrups. I know I wouldn't.

We'd keep then beautifully, thought Katie. And she saw a saddle with gleaming stirrups on the chair in her bedroom, a bridle hanging on the back of her door.

"A saddle costs £50, even an old one," announced Mick, turning away from the paddock. "£50!"

"Some people pay that for a cardigan just one cardigan," Katie said, wiping her eyes. "Really they do. I wonder what her name is. Look, she's coming towards us. Look, she's got a lovely stick. A proper riding one."

Mick turned, though he didn't want to see the girl. Nobby was walking with pricked ears, and she rode easily. Her stirrups glinted in the late afternoon sunlight, her reins were plaited, and Nobby looked different now: he seemed suddenly to have come awake, to be young, instead of old, hollow-backed, bad-tempered.

The girl was waving her stick at them.

"She's angry," Katie said.

"Don't be a twit. He's our pony, more than hers," Mick replied.

28

All the same Katie suddenly felt small and scruffy. She wiped her eyes again, pushed her hair behind her ears.

"We've got as much right here as she has—more," exclaimed Mick as though to convince himself.

"You're trespassing," said the girl, suddenly in front of them. "There's no right of way here."

She had straight, steadfast blue eyes, Katie noticed, a small mouth, a firm chin. She seemed to be looking through them. "It's private here," she said.

And though they had every right to be there, for a moment they were dumb and simply stood staring stupidly at the girl's well-cut clothes. Katie thought suddenly, supposing Mr Stone doesn't really want us to be here? Perhaps he didn't want us to ride Nobby. He wasn't very friendly.

Mick stared at the girl and felt hate and jealousy surging within him.

"We live here," he announced. He wanted to say so much more, to cry, "And Nobby belongs to us as much as to you. Mr Stone has given us permission to ride him as much as we like. He's not yours." But the words wouldn't come.

"So leave us alone," he added lamely instead.

"Well, if you really live here, I suppose it's all right," the girl said. She had a maddening voice, her "here" sounded like "heaar." "I shouldn't lean on the railings anyway. Sometimes there are cows in here and they may have ringworm. You can catch it off fences," she added, as though determined to score off them. "It's a horrible complaint. You have to have your head shaved."

"I know. I'm going to be a vet," said Mick.

"A vet?"

"That's right."

"You must be brainy."

"He is," said Katie.

"Well, that's more than I am. You're leaning on the fence again. Oh well, if you get ringworm, it's your funeral. Come on Tomtit."

She rode away while they stood and stared.

"Tomtit!" exclaimed Katie. "But it's Nobby."

"I expect she didn't like the name—like us. She got in first and called him Tomtit," said Mick wearily, and suddenly his fighting spirit had gone and he wanted to go home and lie on his bed and try to sort his life out, to fit it together again until it was whole like a completed jigsaw.

"Why didn't you say, we had been told we could ride Nobby?" Katie asked.

"Why didn't you?"

"I was so surprised."

The girl had disappeared; the sunlight had gone.

"We'll ride him tomorrow. I'm not going to give up," Mick said.

"Supposing she's riding?"

"We'll tell her to get off."

Katie thought, we won't. We're what Americans call yellow.

"We'd better go back. We promised we'd help Dad. Don't you remember?"

They started to walk back. "I hate this bridle. The blinkers look so silly," Mick said, shaking the bridle contemptuously.

"All the same, it's better than nothing," answered Katie. "Somehow we've got to get some proper tack. I don't know how, but somehow," Mick said, and his mind forged ahead to where they stood at a sale grasping ten pound notes in their hands bidding, "Fifty, sixty, seventy pounds for a saddle."

The auctioneer said, "Name, please?" and he answered loudly, "Michael Smallbone, sir." But they weren't at a sale; they were home, and their father was saying, "How about that digging you were going to do, Mick?" And the twins were screaming in the kitchen; and Mick supposed that the girl was still riding Nobby.

"A girl was riding the pony, Dad," he muttered.

"Perhaps Mr Stone said she could," his father answered.

"He did," said Katie, and saying that seemed to be accepting defeat. She walked listlessly into the kitchen and got out the tea things.

"Two more days to school," said Mrs Smallbone.

"We need a saddle," cried Mick.

"That's a lot of money," replied Mr Smallbone.

"Fifty pounds," Katie said, looking at her brother both knowing the other realised too the uselessness of wanting.

"Perhaps next year. Let's see how the garden does," said Mrs Smallbone.

Mick and Katie looked at one another and Katie saw the days passing, summer turning to autumn, autumn to winter, spring coming, the birds building nests, and they'd ask again and Mum would say the same, "Wait a bit; perhaps next year. Let's see how the garden does."

And one year the strawberries would be disappointing and the next the lettuces, and gradually they would grow and Mick would go the Grammar School, and suddenly they would have outgrown Nobby and they'd never have another chance to ride a pony.

Mick said, "Dad, couldn't you pay us £1 an hour for working in the garden? We could save then."

"It would take many of those £1 coins to buy a saddle." said Mrs Smallbone, putting three spoonfuls of tea into the teapot.

"We'll just have to ride bareback, then," Mick said.

Katie knew then that they weren't giving up, that tomorrow they'd be back in the paddock trying to catch Nobby.

"We'll try sitting on a sack," Mick said, and there was hope again in his voice. "We'll go early before the girl comes," he whispered to Katie. She caught his mood and hope came back to her too, and she thought, unless we move, we've got the whole summer ahead. Surely that will be long enough, and she saw them learning to jump bareback, building the jumps, legging each other up on to the bay pony. And today their father seemed more hopeful too. "The lettuces will be ready next week, and if the weather's good there should be a good crop of peaches come the summer," he said.

"Do you think you'll be able to make a go of it?" asked Mrs Smallbone, putting sugar into the teacups.

"There's a chance at any rate, though only time will show," he answered.

Chapter Four

LET'S MAKE A BARGAIN

So next morning Katie and Mick rose at six thirty, when the sun was already brightening the fading dawn.

They met in the kitchen. "We must be first today," said Mick.

"I bet she doesn't get up till eight," Katie replied. They buttered themselves some bread and ran through the walled garden munching. The dawn had gone; the sky was chequered with cloud. The garden smelt of newly dug earth damp with dew.

Nobby was grazing when they reached the paddock.

"Let's call him Tomtit too, like the girl," suggested Katie.

"All right," agreed Mick.

"Come on, Tomtit," called Katie hopefully.

The pony turned away; the children's hearts sank. He hates us, thought Katie; he knows we're beginners. He scorns us; there are those awful children again, he thinks. She felt suddenly depressed, devoid of hope. Mick was hiding the driving bridle behind his back. If that girl can catch him so can we, he told himself, but he didn't really believe it. She's an expert, he thought. Probably she was riding before she could walk. She probably brings a bucket of oats and she has a proper saddle and bridle. He had dreamed all night of a saddle and bridle; they had hung them in the sitting room feeling as though they had everything they had ever wanted. They had stood and stared, feasting their eyes; then he wakened to an April dawn and to reality; but the feeling of the dream was still with him. He looked at his sister, small, slim Katie, who had left her hair unbrushed.

"Did you remember to bring anything—carrots?" he asked.

"No, I forgot, but I've got a crust of bread."

"I suppose that's better than a poke in the eye with a blunt stick," replied Mick, using one of his father's phrases.

"I wish he liked us," said Katie, seeming to grow smaller and more childlike. "Really I do."

"Perhaps we ought to ring up David Smith. Perhaps he could help us," Mick said.

"It seems awful to be always bothering people," Katie replied, following the bay pony, trying to edge into his line of vision so that he could see the crust of bread she held in her hand.

We're always begging for something, she thought. First it was for a pony to ride; now it's for tack and advice.

"We ought to get a book," she said. "A big fat one all about horse management."

"They're so expensive."

"We might try the library," said Katie.

The dew had soaked through Katie's trainers, so that now her feet felt wet and cold.

"Oh Tomtit, you are a beast. Tomtit, come on," she said. She felt like throwing her piece of bread away, going home in time for breakfast with her parents and the twins in the kitchen, which would smell of bacon and toasting bread. "Look, Tomtit. Can't you see?" she cried, but at the same time she knew he didn't want to see, because a crust of bread wasn't a fair exchange for being ridden by two feeble children.

His ears were back, his eyes sullen. His quarters turned towards her; he was mildly threatening.

"We'd better drive him into a corner," cried Mick, who could see hours passing like an express train. "Get a stick. Come on. It must be breakfast time already. That girl will be here soon. We must catch him."

"We should coax him," answered Katie, but Mick was already searching for suitable sticks. "We've tried coaxing. Don't you want to ride?" he said.

He handed Katie a stick. "Come on. We'll drive him into that corner," he cried, already waving his arms, while Katie felt suddenly sad, thinking, I'm sure this is wrong. He's only a dumb animal, after all.

Mick shouted, "Move on, Nobby. Come on, get cracking." And the pony started to trot, and Katie said, "I thought we decided to call him Tomtit."

"Come on, Tomtit, then," shouted Mick, waving his stick. The pony lumbered away at an unbalanced trot until he drew near the corner; he hesitated for a moment, and Mick cried, "Wave your stick, Katie," as the pony turned, trotted towards her with mouth open, ears back. But Katie only felt fear; she stared at his open mouth; she flung her stick down and ran and at the same moment heard a voice calling, "What on earth are you doing? That's not the way to catch a pony."

She thought, I could die of shame. Fancy running away! I wish we had never set eyes on Nobby, really I do. Then she looked at the girl, who was wearing riding clothes again and held her leather-covered riding cane under her arm.

"Why do you want to catch him, anyway. He's not yours. He's Mr Stone's," she said, and suddenly her voice seemed like authority, like a schoolmistress saying, "What are you doing with Mary's exercise book, Katie?" like an angry householder crying, "Stop rattling my gate, or I'll call the police." Like a land-lady saying, "No, I won't have a piano in my house. What an idea!"

The girl was suddenly one more person who had the power to say, "You can't have that," and so Katie remained speechless, waiting to see what Mick would say.

"He's not yours, either. We have permission to ride him. We've had it for ages," Mick said, and he stared the girl in the face, and saw that she was uncertain now, wondering whether he lied or not.

"So mind your own business," added Mick.

"But it is my business. I'm riding him today. I'm going to the rally," said the girl. "Anyway, since you can't catch him, you can't ride him, can you?"

"What rally?" asked Katie.

"Give us your oats and we'll soon catch him," Mick said.

"What are your names?" asked the girl, and Mick was sure that she meant to check up on them, to ring up Mr Stone and say, "Did you really give a scruffy boy and a girl permission to ride Nobby?" and he loathed her for it.

"Mick and Katie Smallbone. What's yours?" he snapped.

"Paula Ridge. I live half a mile from here in a Tudor cottage; that's its name, in fact. Where do you live?"

"Right here. In the lodge. We run the garden," Mick replied.

They stood staring at one another, blue eyes facing brown. Like two angry dogs about to fight, thought Katie. Tomtit was grazing again, unaware of the conflict he was causing. The dew had dried on the grass; day had come in earnest—a delightful April day.

"Well, I'm jolly well riding him today. I've got my sandwiches packed and everything," said Paula. "How can you ride him if you haven't a saddle and only that awful old driving bridle? anyway, I don't think you can ride."

"Yes, we can. We had a pony once called Prince. At least that's what we called him," Mick said.

And now he's telling lies, thought Katie. Prince was never ours. We only found him and he was called Blue Grass.

"So please move out of my way. I'm late as it is, and I've got to groom Tomtit," Paula said.

"Why should you? You rode him yesterday. It's our turn today," cried Mick.

"But you haven't any tack. That horrible bridle's green with age. You can't possibly ride him in that; it's got blinkers. And he's awful bareback. I know because I tried."

Katie saw suddenly that Paula was pretty, with her dark hair, her high cheek bones and her large blue eyes.

"We are going to ride him. It's our turn," said Mick. "We've hardly ridden him so far, and we start school on the day after tomorrow."

"There's still the evenings. If you're going to the village school, you don't have prep like me. Come on, let me pass," cried Paula.

"No thanks," Mick said. "Come on, Katie. It's our turn." He grabbed the bucket of oats, walked across the paddock calling, "Come on, Tomtit. Co'up."

"This is ridiculous," cried Paula. "I shall fetch Mr Stone."

And he will decide in her favour, thought Katie bitterly.

Mick was bridling Tomtit. "We will have disappeared by the time you return," he replied. "I knew we could catch him if we had oats. I said so, didn't I?"

Paula put down her tack and Katie saw that a tear was trickling down her cheek. She felt mean then. She thought, we're fighting two against one. That isn't fair, really isn't it. "We'll only ride for a bit, Paula," she said. "Then you have him."

"But I'm supposed to be at the rally by ten. Can't you have him tomorrow? You can have my tack. I'll help you catch him. I'm not doing anything," Paula replied, and found a silk handkerchief with a dog embroidered on it and wiped away her tears.

"That is an idea," said Mick, halting Tomtit beside Paula and Katie. "You really mean it? Let's make a bargain."

"All right. But I shan't watch you riding. Your riding will probably make me sick," Paula replied, screwing up her small nose.

"Even you must have started riding some time," replied Mick rudely. "That's definite, is it? You'll meet us here about nine tomorrow with your tack and a bucket of oats . . ."

"All right. I haven't anything else to do. Now give me Tomtit. There isn't time to groom him. I'll have to take him as he is, though what Miss Blenheim will say I don't know." Paula snatched off the driving bridle. She flung it on the ground and produced her own egg-butt snaffle bridle. Mick picked up the saddle.

"You'd better let me do that. You're sure to get the girths twisted," said Paula.

Presently Paula was mounted, riding away without looking back along the shady drive.

Mick started to whistle. "Don't," cried Katie. "We've been so rude."

"What are you talking about? We've more right to Tomtit than she has, nasty little snob."

"Mick, how can you?"

"You're daft."

"I'm not."

Mick started to whistle The Runaway Train. "We're going to ride properly tomorrow," he cried. "We'll really ride." He started to run towards the walled garden. Suddenly the day matched his mood. "This is the beginning," he cried. "Once we start riding everything else will follow."

Chapter Five

LEARNING TO RIDE

The next day was a day which Katie and Mick would never forget. It dawned fine and fair and warm to match their mood. They had spent yesterday afternoon helping their father in the garden—digging and hoeing, going to the door, when Mum was out, to sell two lettuces to a thin lady with glasses and later two bunches of radishes to a tall boy. Life suddenly became how they had dreamed it would be in the past when everything was still uncertain.

The twins had played in the garden among the white daisies growing at random on the green lawn. They had all eaten spring onions fresh from the garden for tea. And, best of all, Dad had started to talk about day old chicks. "We'll buy fifty and you two kids can look after them," he had said, and Katie had seen chicks in her imagination, small and fluffy, and Mick had seen the notice outside the gate, New-laid, Free Range Eggs, and had thought, we'll keep proper accounts, and what we make can buy a really good hen-house if Dad agrees.

They had gone to bed full of hope and speculation. They had wakened early, Katie to creep downstairs and get breakfast, Mick to sit in bed planning—Katie must ride first today, we will make a definite arrangements with Paula; we must groom Tomtit every evening after school. Later they had eaten a good breakfast and still had time to help Mum with the washing-up before setting out for the paddock, their pockets bulging with crusts of bread and apple peel. Mick whistled, hands in pockets; birds flew lazily in the sky.

"It's really spring today," Mick said.

"Supposing Paula doesn't come?"

"Of course she will come."

He had the feeling that today nothing could go wrong, and sure enough when they reached the drive it was to see Paula sitting on the railings swinging her legs.

"At last," she said. She was untidier today, in faded jeans, a red sweater and trainers. "Here are the oats," she continued, holding out a bucket. "You catch him."

A Boxer dog sat beside her. "What's his name?" asked Katie as Mick crossed the paddock whistling and rattling the bucket.

"Sinbad. He's Dad's really. Sit down, Sinbad."

"He's lovely," Katie said.

Tomtit whinnied when he saw the oats, and Mick had the feeling again that today nothing could go wrong.

He put Paula's plaited reins over the pony's head and led him back to where the two girls sat on the railings chewing grass.

"Can't you put it on? I'll do it for you," offered Paula.

"I'm not much good at it," said Mick, suddenly

humble as well as surprised by Paula's good nature. They all saddled the pony, Paula explaining that the girths mustn't cross.

"Who's riding first? Do you know how to mount?" asked Paula.

"It's Katie's turn," Mick answered.

And suddenly Katie wished it wasn't. I shall make a fool of myself, she thought and Paula will kill herself laughing. She saw now that the Boxer was watching her and for a second everyone seemed to be waiting for Katie to mount. Then Paula started to explain. "There are two ways to mount, the English and Continental. Personally, I face the head because I find the other way I stick my toe into Tomtit's stomach."

She demonstrated, and then Katie took the reins and after a short struggle found herself in the saddle.

Paula adjusted her stirrups. "Do you know anything about the aids?" she asked, and gave a long explanation.

"I've never ridden with a saddle before," said Katie, feeling self-conscious. Paula led her up and down talking endlessly.

"Use your legs all the time, each in turn, in time with his walk. Heels down. If you look down, you should only be able to see the tip of your toe. That's better. Sit further forward in the saddle. Shorten your reins."

And every second Katie felt more at home, as though suddenly she knew how to ride.

"We won't trot today," said Paula after a time.

"You're not good enough. See if you can follow me."

And Katie found herself steering Tomtit round the paddock and, because she was sitting properly with her legs in the right place, suddenly it was easy.

"I think it's Mick's turn," said Paula at last, and Katie, shouting "Thank you," took her feet out of the stirrups and dismounted, feeling as though she was descending from the clouds to earth.

Mick had watched carefully. Now he mounted without fumbling and Paula, looking at him, thought, one day he will be good. They both will if it comes to that.

Mick followed Paula's instructions and felt Tomtit walking with a longer stride, felt his head coming up, his whole carriage improving, and suddenly Mick didn't care if he did nothing but walk for days, because he only wanted to learn, to know the secrets of equitation, so that one day he would ride as effortlessly and easily as Paula and David Smith.

But at last Paula said, "I think that's enough for today, otherwise you'll be stiff, and anyway, Tomtit had a hard day yesterday. Tomorrow it'll be my turn. Do you want to borrow my saddle the evening after that? You'll be back at school by then."

Mick dismounted. He thought, we're really learning to ride. It's quite different if you know the aids; it's like learning a whole new language. Happiness swept through him like a sudden warm breeze; he started to pat Tomtit, while Katie said, "Yes, please. We'd love to borrow your saddle. Will you come and teach us again?"

"I'll try to. I'll leave the tack here and some oats in

a bucket, unless it's raining. If it's wet, you'd better come to our cottage. You keep on along the drive, past the big house; then you'll see Tudor Cottage across the other side of the road. It's a pity you haven't got proper riding things; it would make it much easier," Paula said, looking at Mick's newly mended shorts and Katie's old jeans and trainers. "However, perhaps you'll be able to get some later on."

"We're going to keep hens. Perhaps they'll pay for them," Mick replied hopefully.

"We'll buy your eggs; that is if they're free range," Paula said.

They turned on Tomtit. Paula picked up her tack. "Well, be seeing you," she said.

"Yes, and thank you. It's been lovely, really it has," cried Katie.

They watched her walking away with Sinbad at her heels.

"She's nice after all," Katie said.

"I wonder whether she knows David Smith," mused Mick.

"I expect so. Everyone does," Katie said.

They stood leaning against the railings dreaming of the future, neither wishing to move for fear of breaking the spell of happiness which had been over them all morning.

"We'd better go. Perhaps Dad's got the chicks," said Katie at last.

They called "Goodbye, Tomtit," but he didn't raise his head.

"Perhaps he'll like us soon," Katie said.

"When we can ride well, speak his language," Mick answered. "After all, we don't like teachers we can play up, not really, and I reckon ponies are just the same."

He started to whistle again. "Somehow we must get riding clothes," he said.

The walled garden was very warm and sunlit when they reached it, and for the first time Mick felt that here they belonged, that this was their home, their niche in the world.

And, as though to make the day perfect, when they reached the house they could hear a chorus of cheeps.

"He has! He's got the chicks!" cried Katie.

Their parents were bending over two boxes filled with small, fluffy chicks looking as though they had just stepped off an Easter card.

"Come and look," cried Mr Smallbone. "How do you like these?"

Later, when the chicks were installed in the cloak-room, warmed by the electric heater, the family ate Mick's favourite lunch—shepherd's pie followed by treacle tart.

"Well, I saw you riding. Who was the girl?" asked Mr Smallbone.

"Paula Ridge. She's ever so nice," Katie answered.

"She comes from Tudor Cottage. She's got a Boxer dog. She's lending us her saddle," Mick said, and the thought suddenly made him feel happy again, so that he wanted to burst into song, sitting there at the table.

"You be careful of it, then," said Mrs Smallbone.

"We will," they promised, and the future seemed to stretch before them, unbelievably wonderful.

A day later Mick and Katie started school, and though at first they were misfits, it didn't matter because there were the evenings to look forward to; and their rides mattered more and more until they became the highlight of each day, overshadowing all else.

They would come out of school, and instead of walking arm in arm and giggling like most of the other children, they would begin to run, and wouldn't stop until they reached the drive, the railings and sometimes Paula waiting for them. And then their dream would become reality, and each day they seemed to ride a little better. Now, even without Paula, they could catch Tomtit—in fact, often he was waiting for them, his long ears pricked. And he didn't appear ugly to them any more; his long, solemn face seemed beautiful; thanks to the spring grass, his sides were rounder, his neck thinner. Paula had had him shod, and his hoofs looked round and neat. Mick and Katie grew to love him as April turned to May.

Tomtit was so much in their thoughts that their mother constantly exclaimed, "You and that old pony. He's not yours either; he's Mr Stone's."

But he felt like theirs, as though he belonged to them and to Paula Ridge. He featured in all their plans. "When we're rich we'll buy him a summer sheet; a bag of oats. We can't go away for a holiday, Mum, because of leaving Tomtit," they said.

They talked about Paula too. "She seemed so disagreeable at first, but really she's nice; one of the nicest people we've ever met," Mick said.

"Yes; really she is," Katie agreed.

And Paula was full of plans. "When you're better you must ride in shows and join the Pony Club," she told them. "Why don't you get a dog? I'll let you know when I hear of some puppies going." Gradually they talked about Paula as much as they did Tomtit, so that their mother said, "Oh, you and that Paula. why don't you ask her to tea one day, so that the rest of us can give her a look over?"

But they didn't, perhaps because they wanted to keep her to themselves, perhaps because they thought she wouldn't get on with their parents and their spell of happiness would be broken. So gradually May turned to sultry June; their father bought two Wessex sows; the chicks sported wings; the fields and trees were richly green; and then suddenly without warning their spell was snapped.

Chapter Six

YOU WON'T SEE ME ANY MORE

The day was Friday; there was still the whole week-end to look forward to, and the following week was half-term. They came out of school into a sunlit evening. The tarmac was sticky beneath their shoes; flies buzzed round a herd of cows; a dog lay asleep on the concrete outside a garage. It was just like a great many evenings; only possibly more beautiful, more sunlit, more golden with the light of early summer. The other children called after Katie and Mick, "What's the hurry? You and that flipping pony." They knew that they had failed to make friends, but they didn't care, didn't want friends as long as they had Tomtit and Paula, and the heavy-jowled Boxer, Sinbad. The other children laughed at their accent, sometimes accused them of being stuck-up—especially Mick, who was nearly always top of the class.

But that didn't matter either. On this sunlit June evening all that mattered was that they were to see Paula, were to ride. It was too hot to run, but they walked very fast. They didn't talk, because there was no need to—they each knew how the other felt.

The village was nearly empty of traffic; from gardens came the chink of tea-cups; in the sky a plane droned lazily, and Mick imagined the pilot sitting in his seat, basking in the sunlight burning through the fuselage. But Mick was too lazy to think much, what thoughts he had were all happy, as sunny and golden as the day.

They reached the paddock, and there was Paula sitting on the railings as usual, swinging her legs. Then they realised that somehow she was different. She didn't hail them; she sat there as though she didn't care about anything any more. She had been their pillar of strength for so long that they could only stare, and then they saw that she was crying, and that was unbelievable. Suddenly Mick's heart started to thud against his ribs. He could only think, Paula's crying. She's crying. It was something he had never imagined happening. He couldn't believe it now, though he could see the tears streaming down her face; and she just sat there swinging her legs.

He found his handkerchief which was clean. "Have this," he said.

Katie thought, perhaps her parents have been killed in a road accident; something dreadful must have happened. As the weeks had passed she had put Paula on a pedestal—Paula knew everything; she knew how you should sit on a pony; she knew the points of a horse; she could make Tomtit do almost anything she wanted, and now Paula was crying. Katie found her handkerchief and wiped her eyes as though it was she who was crying instead of Paula. And all the sunlight seemed to have gone from the day now.

"Well, there's no need to stare so. I bet you cry sometimes," exclaimed Paula.

And they both looked guilty, as though they shouldn't be there watching Paula cry.

"What's happened? What's wrong?" asked Katie.

"Everything. It's the end of everything. It's my own fault. I've been more or less expelled. I'm going to a new school after half-term—to a boarding school for girls who don't fit in at other schools. You won't see me any more. I'm not to see you again. Now do you understand?" she cried, jumping off the railings, turning her tear-stained face away so that they couldn't see it.

They didn't know what to say. Mick kicked a stone. Katie suddenly saw what it meant—no more riding lessons, no more Sinbad, perhaps no more tack. She thought about the meaning of expelled, and it seemed to belong to a certain collection of words—'stealing', 'lying', 'juvenile court', 'probation'. Paula was facing them again now.

"Why don't you say something?" she cried.

"Do you mean a special school?" asked Katie.

"Yes. I've been leaving early for ages. I hate school. I haven't been trying. I'm always bottom so what's the point? Then, I wanted to help you. I'm no good at making friends. I really haven't any besides you." Paula was still crying and Mick couldn't help thinking, is this really happening? It seemed incredible that only a few minutes had passed since they had been hurrying along the road from school, full of happy thoughts.

Sinbad's eyes never left Paula's face. Mick saw now that she hadn't brought the tack, and he thought, "Oh well, we had to stand on our feet some time; it always seemed too good to last."

51

Katie was saying, "You shouldn't have, Paula. Really you shouldn't."

"Shouldn't have what?" Mick asked. He saw that Paula had stopped crying; she was stroking her Boxer dog and not looking at anything in particular.

"Shouldn't have left school early to help us," Katie replied.

"It's not as simple as that. I wanted to leave school early, anyway; you were just my excuse to myself. I wrote notes pretending they were from Mum. She runs a cafe in town, and she didn't know anything about the notes until the Headmistress, Miss Matthews, rang her up today."

"Was she furious?" Mick asked.

"Yes."

Mick tried to imagine what his father would say if he or Katie were expelled; he would hate to have to go to a special school for backward and difficult boys and girls.

He was getting used to the idea of doing without Paula now, already making plans. Katie was thinking, poor Paula. Really, it's our fault. If she hadn't met us, this might never have happened.

"So you'll have to manage without my tack. It's going to be locked up. But you will be able to have Tomtit all the time. That'll be something, won't it?"

Katie was thinking, she says we're her only friends, and that seemed extraordinary. She thought, surely she has boyfriends. She's pretty, really she is.

"I'd better be going," Paula said. "I've stayed too long as it is."

"We're very sorry," Mick said. "We shall miss you

52

so much. Not just the tack, but you and Sinbad. Won't we Katie?"

"Yes, very much," said Katie and suddenly it seemed as though they had known Paula for years.

"You're our only friend," Mick said.

"Well, now's the time to make some nicer ones," replied Paula, beginning to walk away down the drive.

"You're the only person we know who understands about horses," Mick said, and suddenly he felt inadequate, as though he was attempting a part too old for him. He wanted to say so much, but the words wouldn't come; he couldn't explain how he felt, and all the time Paula was walking away down the drive with tears trickling down her cheeks. "Perhaps you'll like the school," he suggested at last, but it wasn't what he wanted to say at all.

"I shan't. I hate school."

"There may be a nice teacher," suggested Katie.

"There won't be Tomtit."

"Can we write to you?"

"If you like."

"Can we have your address?"

"I don't know it yet."

She spoke as though she wanted to create a barrier between them. And the Smallbone children stopped as though she had said, "Go away, I don't want to talk to you ever again."

"Well, goodbye and thank you for everything," Mick said.

"Yes, thank you," echoed Katie.

Paula did not look back, and her dog followed her

solemnly, as though he knew everything and was in the depths of despair.

Mick and Katie said nothing for a long time. They stood trying to put their thoughts in order, to foresee a future without Paula.

"Well, we may as well ride," said Mick at last.

"It's getting late. We mustn't be long," Katie answered. There was no bucket of oats, no tack, not even a halter.

They saw now the enormous gap Paula's departure was to make for them. They had become accustomed to an elegant saddle and bridle; now they must return to a bridle with blinkers, to riding bareback, to teaching themselves to ride.

"Perhaps we'd better leave it tonight," said Mick, suddenly disheartened.

"There isn't much time left," agreed Katie.

"It was bound to happen," Mick said.

"I don't see why."

"It was all too perfect," said Mick without bitterness.

They walked homewards without noticing the beauty of the evening.

"We've still got the chickens to feed," Mick said.

"I wish they'd start laying."

They could hear Radio 1 broadcasting the latest hits long before they reached the kitchen. Their mother stood waiting for them.

"Come on. It's tea-time," she called.

There was a slab of cheese, a plate piled high with bread and butter, cakes and biscuits and a bowl of rhubarb left over from lunch.

The twins were in their high chairs, waving spoons impatiently and calling, "Mum."

"What's the matter, Katie? You've been crying," their mother said.

"It's Paula. She's being sent away to school," Mick said; and suddenly he didn't want any tea. He saw Paula sitting on the railings in faded jeans swinging her legs; he saw her standing in the middle of the paddock calling. "Toes up, Mick. Shorten your reins. That's better. Well done, Mick," She had encouraged them as much as she had scolded them. And she had dusted their clothes when they fell off, and helped them on again. And she's not to see us again, he thought. "Her tack's locked up. She's going away." He looked at the laden table with disgust. "I don't want any tea, Mum. I want to go upstairs. I think I've got a headache coming," he said, passing a hand across his eyes to wipe away the image of Paula.

"And now it's you. Stop crying, Katie. There's a dear. You can't miss tea. Whatever next, Mick?" cried Mrs Smallbone. "You'll see Paula again. Bad pennies always turn up again."

"She's not bad," shouted Mick, and then stood amazed at the tone of his voice, that he should be standing in the kitchen defending Paula.

"She's good, really she is," said Katie, sitting down at her place.

"Mum, Mum, Mum," screamed the twins.

"Now sit down all of you and eat some tea. You're being silly, really you are. And here comes your Dad."

"And we haven't fed the chickens," said Mick.

"Leave them till after. They won't hurt," said Mrs Smallbone.

Mick sat down, looked at the food and found suddenly that he could eat, that already he was getting used to the thought of life without Paula.

Katie wiped her eyes.

"Can I have a cup of tea. Mum—a real strong one?" she asked.

Life will go on even without Paula, thought Mick. One must never give in. He put some cheese on his plate, passed his cup to his mother; and already the image of Paula was receding a little, growing fainter.

Chapter Seven

DRIVING TOMTIT

Mick wakened early. He thought, something's wrong. Then he remembered—Paula wasn't to see them any more. He lay and thought about it, while outside birds sang. Presently he heard the twins crying and got up. An early morning stillness hung over the house; Better feed the chicks, thought Mick.

Katie heard the twins crying. She went to their room. "Lie down, there's good girls. Mum will be along soon," she told them.

She felt listless, as though the day ahead held nothing for her. She thought, what's the matter with me? before she remembered. It's Paula. She's been sent to a school for bad girls, she thought. What had Paula written in her notes, she wondered, going down to the kitchen to put on the kettle. She felt depressed now. We'll never get a saddle. How can we? she thought. She started to brush her hair. She could hear Mick outside talking to the chicks as though they were human. And we'll be eating some of them soon, thought Katie. Life is awful.

Mick came into the kitchen; he washed his hands. He didn't want to talk, to discuss anything until it was all straight in his own mind. "We'll manage all right," he said at last.

"You mean without any tack?"

"We'll have to, won't we?"

He felt cross now. Other children don't have these difficulties, he thought.

"Can't we try David Smith?" suggested Katie.

"I suppose we could."

"Let's ring him up tonight after school," said Katie.

They saw hope on their horizon again as they stood in the kitchen. Mick laid breakfast in an absent-minded fashion.

They imagined David arriving with a saddle under his arm, a bridle round his neck.

"Even if he hasn't got a saddle, he may know of one," said Mick.

"Sure to," agreed Katie.

"If only we had money, we could have lessons from him, proper ones. Wouldn't that be fantastic?"

"Fantastic," agreed Katie.

"Poor Paula. We'll miss her, won't we? Even if we get another saddle and bridle."

"Yes," replied Katie. "And we didn't like her at first—that's the funny part. Do you remember?"

"Yes, said Mick, remembering her hair, the way it fell forward over her eyes.

"Don't let's talk about her. Let's change the subject," he said.

They had forgotten it was Saturday.

After breakfast they stood discussing what to do. Mick had £1 left over from last week's pocket money. "Let's go to the telephone box and ring up," he suggested.

"When shall we ride?" Katie wanted to know.

Mr Smallbone stood looking at them. "Listen, kids, Mr Stone doesn't feed that pony just for you. It's time he did some work delivering vegetables. Catch him this morning and we'll try him in harness," he said.

Mick and Katie didn't know what to say. They just stood and stared at one another.

"Can you have him in the garden in half an hour's time?" asked Mr Smallbone, picking up his cap.

"Okay, Dad," answered Mick as his father went out of the kitchen, slamming the door after him.

Somehow it made Tomtit seem less theirs, more Mr Stone's. "We'll have to ring up David later. Coming Katie?" asked Mick.

The dew was still on the grass, on the leaves, on the hedges. Cobwebs glistened wet in the sunlight. The garden smelt of fruit and flowers.

"How long have we been here?" asked Katie suddenly.

"Since March."

"It seems like a hundred years."

They had put chopped carrots in the bottom of the kitchen bucket; Katie carried the halter tied round her waist. The railings looked empty without Paula. Katie couldn't help recalling last Saturday, when they had spent the whole day with her in the paddock. She had talked about jumping then. "You'll be able to start soon," she had said. "Tomtit isn't a great jumper, but he'll be all right to begin on." She had worn a blue shirt and jodhpurs, Katie remembered, and it seemed impossible that she wouldn't turn up today, strolling along the drive with Sinbad at her heels.

As for Mick, he felt as though he had lost something—had left it at home. He kept turning round to say things to Paula before remembering that she wasn't there.

Tomtit came to meet them.

"He's expecting oats," Katie said, and the two children felt like cheats, since there was only carrot in the bucket.

"We haven't any brushes," said Mick when they had haltered Tomtit and were leading him towards the gate.

"We'll need such a lot of things now," Katie answered.

In the garden Mr Smallbone was waiting. The cart stood on the centre path; it was a plain enough affair, but it had an adjustable seat and a tailboard which could be put up or down. The children felt excited when they saw the cart. Mick imagined them driving into town. Suddenly life seemed better. He thought, we'll clean the harness, make the brass shine. We'll paint the cart, decided Katie. I wish it had rubber tyres. Still, one can't have everything. I hope Dad lets me drive; it can't be very difficult. Perhaps we can take the twins out in it; better than pushing them in the pram, up the bumpy lanes. Tomtit pushed his nose into the collar.

"It's a long time since I was doing this," said Mr Smallbone.

It was fun to be doing something with their father. The image of Paula receded; instead, there was Mr Smallbone saying, "Easy with the crupper. Here, let me fix the breeching."

Mick started to whistle. "Can we paint the cart,

Dad?" asked Katie.

"We'll have to see. Depends on the Guv'nor. Mr Smallbone often called Mr Stone 'The Guv'nor'; whereas Mick and Katie always thought of him as Mr Stone, rather a remote, elderly figure with whom they had no connection, beyond the fact that he owned Tomtit. The words 'The Guv'nor' always brought them back to reality with a start. He owns our house, remembered Katie, and the garden.

"I'll show you how to drive," said Mr Smallbone jumping into the cart. "Come on kids."

Living in the country had tanned his face, made him look younger.

"Here. Stand up, Nobby," he called.

His mood was new to the children; they saw him suddenly in a new light as they climbed into the cart.

"Let's try him round the garden," said Mr Smallbone, shaking the reins.

Presently they were trotting along the road.

"He goes well," said Mr Smallbone.

After a time he let the children take the reins, each in turn.

"I'm hoping you'll be able to deliver vegetables later on to the village shop. Do you think you'll manage, kids?" asked Mr Smallbone, searching in his pocket for a cigarette.

"Manage it?" thought Katie; and she saw them trotting through the village every Saturday, the iron tyres rattling on the tarmac, vegetables piled up behind them.

"Yes, we'll manage all right, won't we Katie?" replied Mick.

And he thought, the garden must be paying. We're going to be here for ever. And he felt like cheering. He thought, perhaps we'll be rich. Perhaps later on we'll have a pony of our own, and Mum can have that fur coat she's always talking about.

He thought how wonderful it would be if he and Katie could ride together through the neighbouring woods, over the downs, which you could see, faint and blue in the distance from the top window in the lodge.

Then they were home, unharnessing Tomtit.

"I've got plans for a mushroom bed later on," said Mr Smallbone.

"How lovely, Dad. I love mushrooms," Katie said.

"We'll have to be getting some oats for old Nobby if he's going to work," he continued.

The children didn't say that they called the pony Tomtit. They left his bridle on and rode him bareback to the paddock, and this time they could look at the railings without missing Paula, because suddenly a new future seemed to stretch before them.

Mick was feeling grown-up; he saw himself helping his father weigh out the vegetables, until he was able to do it himself.

Katie saw the cart painted; endless summer days, bowls of strawberries, baskets of raspberries, a shopping expedition when the whole family had new clothes, the twins pretty dresses, her mother a new coat. And she and Mick would have riding clothes, she thought, seeing herself in a blue skull-cap. And Dad, what would Dad have? A new suit, she supposed.

The children watched Tomtit roll. "Tomorrow we can ride him, Dad says. The next day we're to drive him round to the farm for a bag of oats," said Mick.

"Do you think we can manage that?" asked Katie.

"Of course we can. Driving's dead easy. There's nothing to it. And the next day we're to get out of school as early as we can and get him a new set of shoes."

"You mean at the blacksmith's?"

"Where else? Did you think we'd take him to a shoe shop?"

"I'm not as soft as that."

They started to walk home.

"Do you think Paula will write?" asked Katie. For in spite of everything the paddock and drive still seemed faintly haunted by her, as though part of her remained there watching them.

"I don't know," said Mick, and he tried to ignore his memory of Paula's face, which rose instantly to his mind.

Chapter Eight

DAVID COMES

The next day they rode, taking it in turns, exploring the woods, saying, "Toes up," to one another, imitating Paula. They tried to forget that Tomtit wore blinkers on his bridle but they couldn't forget that they were bareback. They had telephoned David the night before. Katie, suddenly shy, said, "You speak, Mick," though it had been her idea in the first place.

"Hello. Can I speak to David Smith?" Mick had said, and the two children had waited impatiently while the person who had answered the telephone fetched David.

Mick had explained who they were to David: "We found Blue Grass if you remember and you put us in touch with Mr Stone."

"Of course I remember you, Mick. What can I do for you?" asked David politely.

"We haven't got a saddle. That's the trouble," cried Mick and was suddenly embarrassed.

He wished at that moment that Katie had never thought of telephoning. But David was saying, "Well, we have got a spare one. Do you want a bridle too? Let's see, tomorrow's Sunday. I'll come over in the evening. I can't talk now; I'm in the middle of lunging a youngster."

Mick had cried, "Thank you," before the conversation ended.

"There, what did I say? I knew David would help us," Katie had cried in triumph.

Now, riding through cool woods where the ground was as dry as sand is beyond the reach of the sea, they discussed the saddle. "I hope it's got a leather girth," Katie said.

"And stainless steel stirrups," added Mick.

"Did he say what bit the bridle had?"

"No, but it's sure to be a snaffle, isn't it?"

"You mean because we're beginners?"

"Yes, and because most people ride in snaffles nowadays."

"We'll look after it properly; clean it every day," Katie said.

"Of course," agreed Mick.

They each had a canter in a field before they turned for home.

"We're getting much better, aren't we?" said Katie.

"If only we could have lessons. If we had a saddle, we could join the Pony Club, learn to ride properly. But how can we go to one of their rallies bareback with Tomtit in blinkers?" asked Mick. He felt angry now. Were they to ride for ever in borrowed tack on a borrowed pony?

Katie must have guessed how he felt, because she said, "Maybe the mushrooms will earn a lot of money. They're ever so expensive in the shops. Really they are."

"Things take so long," moaned Mick. "First the sheds have to be built then the beds prepared, then the spawn has to be sown or whatever you do with spawn. Then I bet weeks pass before you have any mushrooms."

"You always were in a hurry, Mick," Katie said. "I don't see why you have to be so cross when David's bringing some tack tonight."

She thought, he's cross because it was my idea, not his. Though she was younger than Mick, she suddenly felt older. If he had suggested ringing up David Smith, everything would be all right.

"Anyway, it's my turn now," cried Mick.

At three o'clock the children started to wash. Katie put on her prettiest dress and combed her hair. Mick said, "Where are my best shorts, Mum, and my checked shirt?"

Mrs Smallbone said, "Whatever do you two want to go dressing up for? Here, Katie hold Rachel for a moment, there's a good girl; then perhaps I'll find Mick his clothes."

By three thirty they were ready; but there was no sign of David.

"I thought he was coming this evening," observed Mrs Smallbone, putting a pile of ironing on the kitchen table.

"I'll do that for you, Mum," Katie offered.

"It may not be evening, but he may be early. When does evening start, anyway?" Mick asked.

"After tea," replied Mrs Smallbone, firmly. "You both look very nice I must say, though I say it who shouldn't," she continued. "It's time you started going to Sunday School. You don't seem to have made any friends in the village. You're an odd pair, you are."

Mick and Katie looked at one another, but said nothing. Katie switched on the iron. They felt unsettled. Supposing he doesn't turn up? thought Katie. I hope it's a forward-cut saddle, thought Mick. Teatime came. Katie took the ironed clothes upstairs to the airing cupboard. Mick stood staring out of the window.

"Come on, Mick. Staring out of the window won't bring him here," said Mrs Smallbone.

In the end David came at six o'clock when Katie was helping bath the twins and Mick was feeding the chicks, which were nearly chickens. He came up the path carrying a saddle and bridle and knocked on the front door.

"There he is. Leave the twins and go and open the door," Mrs Smallbone told Katie. I can manage now."

"Mick, he's here," called Katie out of the window before she went downstairs.

She saw now that her hands and the front of her dress were wet. She wished she hadn't changed.

She opened the front door.

"Hello, Katie. I've brought the tack. Can we try it on?" David said. His eyes were browner than she remembered them. He was wearing riding clothes.

"You mean catch Tomtit?"

"Yes, if he isn't already caught."

"That's all right," said Mick, suddenly beside them. "We can catch him; it's no trouble at all."

"But he's some distance away," Katie added, staring at the dark brown saddle David held under his arm.

They walked together through the sunlit garden, and David admired the espalier and fan-trained fruit trees. He stopped when he came to the cart. "Is that Nobby's?" he asked.

"Yes, it needs a coat of paint," Katie answered.

"We call him Tomtit," Mick said.

"You're fond of changing names—Blue Grass to Prince, now Nobby to Tomtit," David said.

"We didn't think of Tomtit. Paula already called him that. Do you know Paula Ridge?" Mick asked. Suddenly it was important that David should like Paula. Mick wished that she could be there tonight, sitting on the railings swinging her legs. They would get on, he thought; they're what Dad calls kindred spirits.

"No, I don't think I do," David said.

They talked about Paula as they walked on towards the paddock, and David didn't judge her. "She sounds nice and a good friend," he said before they were climbing the paddock railings and walking towards Tomtit, while Katie couldn't help thinking, this is really happening—the famous David Smith is here with us, helping us, and because of that the sun seemed to shine brighter, and life was suddenly full of hope and of dreams all destined to come true.

Tomtit whinnied to them, and Katie remembered the way in which he had welcomed them far back in windy March and was suddenly triumphant.

"He hated us at first, really he did," she told David.

They put the halter on Tomtit, and David said, "The bridle will be all right, but I don't like the look of his back much, it's very hollow, isn't it?"

"Yes. But it doesn't seem to matter, really it doesn't. He's very strong," Katie said, as though she was trying to sell the pony whose ears were like a mule's.

"I don't mean that."

"You mean the saddle won't fit," Mick said, and he couldn't keep the wretchedness he felt from his voice. This is just our luck, he thought.

"Yes; look. See, it's right on his withers," David said.

"Couldn't it be changed?" asked Katie in a small voice. "Stuffed or something?"

"I doubt that it could be stuffed enough. Anyway, it's not my saddle. It's just an odd one kicking about the stables. I thought you might as well have it; it's better for a saddle to be used and cleaned than to be left lying about," David explained, while suddenly the evening seemed cooler to the children, as though evening had turned to dusk in one fleeting moment.

"Let's try the bridle, anyway," David suggested briskly, without looking at the Smallbones' small, disappointed faces, which brought back to him too clearly the bad moments in his own childhood.

"The bridle fits all right. Saddles are always tricky. Paula Ridge probably had hers altered to fit him, or bought it with him in view," David said.

They stood looking at the bridle. "It's a lovely one," Mick said at last. "Can we have it for a few weeks?"

"Oh, more than that. It's one of mine. I wish the saddle was too, then I would have it altered for you," David answered, fiddling with the cheek straps.

"We'll keep it very clean," promised Katie.

"Have you any funds? Can you save up for a saddle?" asked David.

"Not really." Mick didn't want to admit that they were supposed to have a pound for pocket money each week, but that his father would forget all about it nine weeks out of ten.

"I wish we could work. But we're too young even for a newspaper round," Mick said.

"But Dad says perhaps next year he'll buy us a saddle," Katie said. She thought, Mick makes us sound so poor; we're not that poor; we're not on Income Support or anything.

"Why don't you get him good at competitions, teach him to bend?" asked David, looking at Tomtit. "The prizes are often money, and if you go to the small local shows you might have quite a chance."

"What, bareback!" exclaimed Mick.

"Yes, even bareback. Let's go back to your house, and I'll write a list of competitions down for you, give you all the details; it's important to have the poles the right distance apart in a bending race, for instance," David said, turning Tomtit loose.

"You mean we're to practise?"

"Of course."

The children started to feel better; suddenly there was hope again, a plan, an ambition to achieve. They saw themselves winning a bending race, felt the thrill of receiving a prize. David seemed happier too. "I think you've done wonders on Nobby, anyway. He looks quite different," he said.

"It was Paula too," replied Mick, wondering suddenly what she was doing at this moment. What did girls do at Special School? he asked himself, and didn't know the answer.

David thought, he likes Paula in the same way as I cared for Pat years ago, and he saw himself small and untidy, going up to her home, The Hall, for the first time. He remembered leaving a dance in the middle; the riding school they had run together; the last time he had seen her, fourteen months ago at Badminton.

"You know you can always count on me to help you in any way," he said climbing the paddock railings. "If you want advice, ring up."

All the same, Mick couldn't help feeling disappointed as they walked back through the garden. Once again they had hoped for too much. Why hadn't they realised that saddles had to fit? He saw months of work ahead of them, and David might be wrong—Tomtit wasn't fast. He might not like bending. He might hate cantering round the ring with other ponies in musical chairs. They all went into the house together, and Mick said, "Mum, this is Mr David Smith," and then wondered whether it would have been better to omit the Mr.

"Glad to meet you, I'm sure," answered Mrs Smallbone, shaking David's hand.

Katie's dress was crumpled where it had dried, and for the second time she wished that she had worn her jeans instead.

Mick, looking round the kitchen for a pencil thought, we haven't the right clothes, anyway. I can't ride at a show in shorts, even if I'm bareback.

"I'll make a list of competitions. You can practise the Potato Race quite a lot on your feet, and the Sack Race if it comes to that.

71

"I've done the Sack Race at school, on Sports Day. I'm ever so good at it, aren't I, Mick?" said Katie.

"What about staying on for a spot of supper?" asked Mrs Smallbone.

"I don't think I'd better, thanks all the same. I'm in charge this Sunday, and that means going round the boxes in an hour's time," David answered.

And now Mick and Katie could think of nothing to say. Katie straightened the front of her dress.

"Well, all the best. I hope to see you on the first Sunday in August at the local show, if not before," David said.

The house seemed somehow empty when he had gone, driving away in a battered old car. "Leaning forward," Mr Smallbone said, "as though he was on a blooming horse."

"He seemed all right; not stuck up at any rate; not like some one could name," commented Mrs Smallbone, and Mick wondered to whom she was alluding.

Katie sat staring at the piece of paper David had written on. He had a neat, clear handwriting, and what he had described seemed to reveal a new world to Katie. She couldn't help wondering whether they would ever reach it. David seemed to think they could, but only yesterday they cantered for the third time. How long would it take them to gallop between bending poles without a saddle? For want of a saddle the race was lost, thought Katie.

Mick still felt disappointed. He said, "What's for supper, Mum?" because he didn't want to think about the problems ahead yet, to face up to the fact that they were still without a saddle, that they were teaching themselves to ride without even a book.

"Cold meat, potato salad and a spot of lettuce," replied Mrs Smallbone, going to the larder.

Chapter Nine

WHAT ARE YOU DREAMING ABOUT?

The children slept badly that night, and wakened late the next morning. They were late at school, and, because of that, late out of school. The day was stifling; the sky completely still, without even a plane to break its cloudless blue. All the same, there was the feeling of thunder in the air, and at times a faint breeze stirred the still green leaves on the trees.

Mick felt cross as he hurried out of school; all day everything had gone wrong; he had been dull and inattentive, bored with the lessons and the teachers.

Katie was hot; her shoes stuck to the tarmac. She thought, we haven't got a saddle. David was really our last hope.

"We'd better bag some of Dad's bean-poles for bending posts," said Mick suddenly, "and they'll do for Musical Poles as well."

Suddenly it seemed to Katie that they had been wanting a saddle for years and years, that it was simply one more thing they would never have. On this hot afternoon, it was impossible to believe that they would ever win a race in a gymkhana, much less enough money to buy a saddle. And other children get given saddles, she thought. Look at Paula. It isn't fair.

"We'd better get the poles first," Mick said. "Where's the piece of paper? You know, the competitions David wrote down for us."

"In my rucksack."

It was seven o'clock before the bending posts were up, and the buckets waiting for the Potato Race. They'd had tea by this time and Tomtit was standing by the railings wearing David's egg-butt snaffle.

The thunderstorm still lurked in the air. "You'd better have first go," Mick said.

He sat on the railings holding a wooden mallet.

"Hurry up. It's late," he said.

Katie rode Tomtit in between the poles while Mick sat on the railings calling, "Faster. That's much too slow," until suddenly hot and tired, she felt tears trickling down her cheeks.

"Here. You have a go. It's not easy," she cried, trotting towards Mick, who still sat swinging the mallet. "I bet you can't make him go any faster. I bet . . ."

"David said he would be good at it, so he must be," cried Mick, as though to convince himself.

They stopped riding at nine o'clock. Walking home through the garden, where the fruit was ripening, they were too disheartened for conversation.

"It takes time, like everything else," was all Mick managed to say, while Katie walked silently, her handkerchief screwed into a ball in the middle of her hand.

She thought, we couldn't even trot between the

poles; and I never got a potato in the bucket, not even once.

"At last," said Mrs Smallbone when they entered the kitchen. "No wonder you can't wake up in the mornings—it's gone nine o'clock. You should be in bed by half past eight."

The children said nothing; Katie wanted to be in bed between clean sheets. She wanted to fall asleep and forget that they hadn't a saddle, that they couldn't make Tomtit bend properly.

"Sorry, Mum," said Mick.

"And your Dad wants you up early tomorrow. He wants you to take some things over to the shop with the pony and cart," said Mrs Smallbone. "Here, have something to eat before you go up, and go quietly. I don't want the twins woken; Rachel's teething, poor little soul."

So next morning they were up early, catching Tomtit, helping their father harness him, trotting through the village past their own school, shut and quiet, past the pond where ducks were still, their bills tucked neatly beneath their wings, on to the shop. A tall, thin woman took the vegetables from them, and Mick remembered to give her the bill, and then they trotted homewards through the bright June morning.

"It's a pity the twins couldn't come. They would have loved it," Katie said.

They both felt better this morning. A good night's sleep had brought them back hope. "We rode too long last night," Mick said letting the pony walk.

"And made him stale and sour," agreed Katie. They couldn't be despondent this morning : the very air seemed to whisper of hope, of races won, ambitions achieved. Mick couldn't stop whistling. We'll give him more oats, he thought, looking at Tomtit, and he saw himself galloping past a finishing post while his parents and Katie cheered and called, "Come on Mick, Mick! Oh, well done Mick."

Today he felt he could achieve anything, even the eleven-plus, which grew nearer and nearer.

That evening they rode again, and the next, and each time Tomtit seemed to go a little better. On the third, Mick said, "The trouble is we can't judge how good he is."

"You mean we can't race him against anyone else, another pony?" asked Katie.

"That's right."

They had turned the bay pony loose and he stood nearby devouring a bucket three-quarters full of oats. Mick and Katie were happy; Katie was thinking, if only life could be always like this, all sun and flowers and riding. She wanted to keep the moment for ever in her memory.

"We ought to join the Pony Club; that's what we ought to do." she said with assurance, because this evening she was full of confidence in herself. I'll be a smashing rider one day, really I will, she thought.

"That's no good, silly. The Pony Club only meets in the holidays. A Riding School's what we want."

"What about David's?"

"It's not really a school; that's the trouble."

"Well, he'd know of one, wouldn't he?"

"Do you think we can ring him up again? we can't keep bothering him."

"He said we should ring up if we wanted advice, didn't he?"

They stood up. Above the downs the sun had set. From far away came the baa of sheep. For a moment they thought they saw Paula coming along the drive; but when the figure came closer they saw it was an old lady with a shopping basket.

"Do you think we'll see Paula again?" Mick asked.

"I don't know."

The old lady had gone now. "Let's ring up David, then," Mick said, beginning to run, because he was trying to forget Paula. She never sent us her address, he thought. She didn't, though she promised to. That wasn't very nice of her, he thought, and suddenly for the first time he realised how the fact had hurt him. For days he had wakened, listened for the postman, gone downstairs, looked on the mat; and she had never written.

"I expect Mum was right," he decided, opening the gate into the garden. "She isn't any good; only bad people get sent to special schools."

Katie was thinking about Paula too. "It's funny we never heard from her; perhaps she wasn't allowed to write to anyone, only home. Poor Paula. Mick doesn't seem to care though, not now, thought Katie. Oh well, it takes all kinds to make a world. I wonder what David will say? Perhaps he'll think it's a cheek us ringing up again so soon."

But when they telephoned David seemed pleased to hear from them.

"He's bending well? Oh, good. Yes, let's see, there's a riding school quite near you; it's run by a Miss Potter; she's really very nice," he said.

Katie was doing the talking; Mick stood beside her trying to curb the excitement he felt rising inside him. A riding school! We're really going to ride at a riding school, he thought.

"I should think Saturday will be the best day. I'll let her know you're coming. I'm sure she won't mind,"David continued.

"Oh, thank you," cried Katie.

"She lives at Deansborough. Do you think you can find it on the map? It's roughly four miles from you," David said.

"Say yes, Katie," cried Mick.

"Her stables are called the White Horse Stables; they're next to a pub of that name."

"Yes; we'll find it, really we will," replied Katie.

A few minutes later she had hung up.

"It's all fixed, everything's fixed. I never thought it would happen," she cried, her voice shrill with happiness.

"You mean us ride with other children? Nor did I," Mick said. They stared at one another, and Katie said, "Oh Mick, I'm so happy."

"We'll probably fall off, and we haven't got a saddle," said Mick with a wide grin.

"And be last in all the races."

"We've got two days; let's give him a rest tomorrow from races; just so he isn't stale."

They sat making plans until their mother called, "Bed-time. Come on. It's gone eight and you've got your exam next week, Mick."

But at this moment the exam held no horrors for Mick, for he was seeing himself cantering round a paddock with other children, his heels down, his hands in the right place, Tomtit going easily, his neck arched, his nose dropped.

He thought, we're going to win prizes like David said, and then one day we'll have a saddle—a saddle we can call our own. Then we'll hunt. He saw a velvety, winter dawn, grey, silver with dew, hounds coming down a village street, and I'll be on Tomtit, he thought, waiting with the others saying, Good Morning Master, as though it wasn't my first hunt as though I had hunted often, was a hard rider to hounds.

Mrs Smallbone called again, "Mick, what did I say? Come along. What are you dreaming about? Not worrying about the exam, are you?"

"No, Mum; not that," Mick said, and now he heard the Gone Away, echoing across bare winter fields. "We're going to a Riding School next Saturday, Mum. David's arranged it," he said, unable to keep the joy he felt from his voice.

"I hope it's all right. Won't you have to pay?" asked Mrs Smallbone.

"He didn't say anything about that, did he, Katie?"

"No, nothing at all. we're only going just the once. Only to try Tomtit against the other ponies, that's all," Katie said. She felt defeated now, flat; after all,

Miss Potter might not want them; it might be raining.

But Mick was still full of hope and plans.

"One day you're going to get a surprise, Mum," he promised. "Come the Show . . ."

Chapter Ten

THE RIDING SCHOOL

And now Mick and Katie could only think of Saturday. It had been like that once before, when they had gone to the Littleheath Stables to meet David; that day had nearly ended in disaster. But they hadn't learned from it. They started counting the hours till Saturday, arguing who would ride first; imagining themselves racing with other children. "Think of something else, Mick. You'll fail your exam, if you don't stop thinking about those stables," complained Mrs Smallbone.

"Your heads are getting swollen," said Mr Smallbone. "You can't spend your lives gallivanting about on Mr Stone's pony."

"We're going to give you a surprise one day, Dad. You wait until the Show," boasted Mick.

"What did I say? The boy's getting a swollen head," said Mr Smallbone.

But they didn't heed their parents, and when at last Saturday came, fine after a wet night, they rose early, met in the kitchen, started for the paddock without a word. And Tomtit whinnied when he saw them, trotted towards the gate with pricked ears, as though he knew it was a special morning. They gave him a feed of oats, groomed him, finished him off with one of their mother's tea towels.

"It's funny. Do you remember how ugly he seemed the first day we saw him? He doesn't seem ugly now," Mick said.

"No. He's beautiful," replied Katie, polishing the bay pony's hind legs. "We need some oil for his hoofs. There's some in the greenhouse. Do you think we can have that?"

"If we don't take much," Mick said.

"I wish Paula could be there, just to see how we've got on. Not that she cares probably."

"Probably not. Funny she never wrote."

They stood for a moment remembering Paula. She had really started all this. How I hated her at first," Mick remembered, "But then afterwards she was different, quite different."

"She must miss Tomtit. And Sinbad, if it comes to that," decided Katie. "Will she be allowed home for the holidays? Supposing she wants Tomtit? What will we do then?"

They walked back to the house for breakfast, and Mrs Smallbone said, "Let's see. This is the morning, isn't it?"

"Yes, that's right," replied Mick.

They washed their faces, combed their hair, wished that they had riding clothes, went out into the sunlight, through the garden to the paddock, to Tomtit who stood where they had left him tied to the railings. It seemed to them that this was the opening of a new chapter in their lives. They felt that there should be a gathering in the drive calling, "Goodbye. Good luck. All the best."

"You ride first," Mick said.

They bridled the pony, started along the drive to the big gates at the end, which gave them direct access to the road. A milk float passed them. Flies buzzed round the pony's ears. A church clock chimed eight. "We're in plenty of time," Mick said.

"We've forgotten our sandwiches."

"Was Mum going to make some?"

"She said so last night."

"Perhaps she forgot."

Mick didn't care about the sandwiches; it was enough that they were going to Miss Potter's Riding School, that they had a pony to ride, and that they planned to ride in a gymkhana.

He knew how he would feel on that great day. Hadn't he watched it all on TV, and felt at home even then inside the ring ropes? One day he would stand there in the centre judging, Michael Smallbone, the well-known vet. He would have a shooting-stick, a cap he wore at a slant; he would be famous.

"Say when you're tired. When you think it's your turn," Katie told him.

But he knew today he could walk for hours without noticing. He started to whistle. "I'm all right," he replied. "I'm not tired at all."

And Katie stayed silent after that, staring into her own future, seeing herself a girl groom, travelling the shows, watching the great riders; going to the Continent with a British team, to America. Only probably Mum wouldn't like it, she thought. It would be, why do you want to work with horses?—be a nanny? You could travel just the same then. As if I hadn't had enough with Rachel and Kelly, thought Katie.

And now the road was strange, and there was more traffic, and presently a river, reflecting the trees which stood on its banks. There seemed to Katie to be beauty everywhere—in the sky where flimsy clouds floated, in the greenness of the trees, in the depths of the slowly flowing river.

They crossed a bridge, stopped to look at a map.

"Here. It's your turn now," said Katie, dismounting.

People were up and about now. Men dug in their gardens, women were shaking mats outside doors, dogs lay in the sun, cats sat on window-sills. They turned left at some crossroads.

"It can't be much more than a mile ahead," Mick said. They were excited now; they started to hurry.

"Isn't it my turn to ride again?" cried Katie.

"If you like," answered Mick, jumping off, throwing his sister the reins, starting to run ahead along the road.

Then suddenly they were there, staring at loose-boxes, at a paddock full of poles, of jumps, of tracks made by many hoofs. For a moment they stood outside, in the road, simply staring. The yard they saw was full of children; the horses and ponies looking over the loose-box doors were of different sizes and colours. And we don't know a bay from a chestnut, thought Katie suddenly. We really know nothing. She was appalled standing there. Why had they come? They had no saddle, no riding clothes, only a borrowed bridle on a borrowed pony. She could see into the saddle room, where bridles hung in rows, where saddles were being removed by children to be put on the backs of ponies. We don't know much, really we don't, she thought.

"We may as well go in. Perhaps I'd better lead him. He may not want to go in," said Mick, who didn't want his sister to make a fool of herself.

Katie dismounted and they entered the yard. Everyone seemed to turn to look at them then—horses, ponies, children, even a fat Labrador dog sitting in the sun.

"I expect you want Miss Potter. She's in the saddle room," said a tall, dark haired boy.

"Haven't you got a saddle?" asked a girl who looked six or seven, and who was advancing on a large pony, a double bridle in her hand.

Katie didn't answer; she was feeling all wrong, out of place. We shouldn't have come. We haven't got the right clothes or anything, she thought. I wish I had never thought of ringing up David, really I do.

"Oh hello," said Mrs Potter, coming out of the saddle-room. "Let's see, you're the Smallbones, aren't you? Oh dear, haven't you got a saddle? David didn't mention that. I don't know whether I can lend you one. Let me think."

She had wispy grey hair, a kind face, grey-green eyes. Her clothes were well-cut and threadbare. Mick, looking at her, was certain that she must know everything there was to know about horses.

"It doesn't matter. We always ride bareback," he said.

"Really we do," agreed Katie.

"I know. There's Pilot—he's lame. It might fit," replied Miss Potter, going back to the saddle-room.

"Now we're being a nuisance," Katie muttered.

"Did you come all the way bareback, really?" asked the small girl.

"Yes, it's only four miles," Mick said.

"Here we are. Let's see if it'll fit," Miss Potter exclaimed.

"He's very difficult to fit; he's got a hollow back," explained Mick.

"This one fits nearly everyone," replied Miss Potter. "Oh dear, he is awkward, isn't he? Look, it's right on his withers. Oh dear, what can we do?"

"We don't mind riding bareback," Mick said.

A crowd of children had gathered round Tomtit and the Smallbones.

"What about Julie's, Miss Potter?" suggested a girl.

"Wouldn't Romany's fit him?" asked a boy called Hugh.

"We don't mind riding bareback, really we don't," Katie said.

"Or Marmite's?"

"Or Piper's?"

Mick and Katie felt hemmed in. Miss Potter passed a hand across her brow. "Oh dear, I don't know. No; not Piper's. Don't be an ass, Ann. Not Marmite's. If only we had a spare numnah, not that they're much fun to ride on but they are better than nothing."

Katie thought, they're pitying us.

"We're used to riding bareback, Miss Potter," insisted Mick. "We didn't expect to be lent a saddle; soon we're going to buy one, but we haven't got round to it yet."

"You will have to have one made for him, I'm afraid. It'll cost you a hundred pounds or more. You know that, don't you?" asked Miss Potter, looking at the Smallbones, as though she knew how poor they were, as though she knew everything. Katie looked at her jeans and was ashamed. Why did we come? Why didn't we wait a bit? Wait until we had proper clothes? she thought.

"We know that, Miss Potter. We reckoned it would be about that," Mick said. He saw now that Tomtit was ugly, for his head couldn't compare in beauty with those that looked over the loose- box doors; his ears were like a mule's, his nose coarse, his neck short, his shoulders straight and, worst of all, his back hollow. We've been living in a dream world, thought Mick, making him beautiful because we couldn't bear him to be ugly. Thinking we could ride, when really we're just untaught beginners.

Now he didn't want to ride with Miss Potter's pupils. He wanted to go home before all his dreams lay shattered. He felt tired and untidy standing in the yard. We don't belong here, he thought; we never will.

The other children were still suggesting saddles. Miss Potter stood with wrinkled brow, saying, " Oh dear, what shall we do?"

Katie muttered, "Let's go, Mick."

Mick pretended not to hear.

Then someone who looked like a girl groom called, "Miss Potter, do you know it's gone ten?"

"Oh Vanessa, it hasn't," cried Miss Potter. "Everyone to horse. Oh dear, now we'll be late all day."

And it's all our fault, thought Katie.

"Let's go, Mick" she said, for the crowd had dispersed, were now engaged in mounting, or in pulling up girths, or in bridling ponies which had been forgotten.

Mick and Katie were suddenly miraculously alone.

"Do you think they're going to ride in the paddock?" asked Mick.

"I suppose so."

Suddenly Katie no longer cared. We might have known this would happen, she thought. Only David boosted us up; he seemed to think we were good enough to come.

Perhaps we'll learn something from watching, thought Mick. At least we can see how fast these ponies bend.

The yard was emptying, the loose box-doors stood open.

"Last through shut the gate," called Miss Potter. "Hurry up, Louise. We're late as it is. Use your legs."

"They're lovely ponies," Katie said. "Like Prince was."

"Don't. You'll offend Tomtit. He's lovely too. Aren't you Tomtit?" Mick said, patting the bay.

"If we had a saddle we could be riding there, too." Katie said.

"It'll be at least a hundred pounds. That's what she said, wasn't it?" cried Katie, as though she knew now that they'd never have a saddle for Tomtit as long as they lived.

"A hundred pounds, so what?" cried Mick.

"It's a lot of money; more than Dad used to earn in a week sometimes," replied Katie, blowing her nose, wiping her eyes, thinking, why did we look forward to today so much? Why don't we learn from experience? Why do we go on struggling?"

"At least we've got a proper bridle now. At least we didn't bring Tomtit in blinkers," Mick said.

Suddenly it seemed to Katie that she had lived for years and years. Their arrival at the market garden seemed to have happened a century ago. There had followed their efforts to catch Tomtit, Paula's appearance, followed by her tuition; that seemed to have happened at least a year before David's appearance on the scene, and yet actually they had arrived with the removal van in March, and now it was July, that made hardly more than three and a half months altogether. And yet I feel years older, thought Katie. The days of foster-parents and Prince seem to belong to another life altogether. I feel at least fourteen.

Chapter Eleven

GYMKHANA ENTRIES

Katie and Mick stood and watched. The children in the paddock rode their ponies round and round the school, which was marked by white posts; they reined back, turned on the forehand and haunches, rode circles. They rode singly and in pairs, cantered each in turn, were corrected and instructed by Miss Potter. Mick and Katie didn't understand it all; but Paula had taught them the turn on the forehand, and they recognised it now; they saw too when a pony was cantering on the wrong leg, and watching, they learned what terms like, "Over bent," "behind the bit," and "going into the ground," meant or near enough. They forgot that they hadn't a saddle while they watched, even that they had meant to be there riding with the others.

"Don't they ride well?" Katie asked. "If only we could ride like that!"

"We will one day; you'll see." Mick could hardly take his eyes off the class; it was like reliving a dream.

When had he dreamed he watched a class? Each of Miss Potter's instructions was transmitted instantly to his memory. It was as though he had always know this moment would come to him. One day . . . one day

. . . his thoughts ran, and a hundred images rushed to his mind, all in some way or other connected with horses or with him being a vet.

Katie stood thinking, I'm glad we've come; anyway, we're learning. We only need money, that's all; money and we would be riding here with these other children.

The class wheeled into the centre of the school and halted, shoulder to shoulder, knee to knee.

"Now we'll have some competitions," Miss Potter announced, walking towards the bending poles.

Katie and Mick looked at each other, and each knew that the other was thinking, if only we had a saddle.

"We'll see how fast they go," said Mick.

"Yes", agreed Katie but really it was no consolation. They were sick with disappointment standing there. We've come so far, Katie thought, and now we can't do what we came for just because we haven't got a saddle. It seems so silly somehow, really it does.

"Let's go in," suggested Mick, opening the gate.

"Do you think she'll mind?" asked Katie, following Mick and Tomtit.

"She won't have to."

Everyone seemed to be looking at them now, and Katie was conscious of her faded jeans, and Mick thought, let them look; one day they'll be able to say, "I remember Mick Smallbone as a boy. He was quite poor then, not famous at all . . ." And they'll be glad they knew me then.

"Do you want to join in? Come on, then. You can race with the beginners," called Miss Potter.

Mick vaulted on to Tomtit. Suddenly he didn't care what anyone thought of him—he was going to race after all.

"Yes, please," he called.

"Your sister can have my pony," said a girl called Judy. "I've gone in for bending races so many times. Katie, would you like to try Curfew?" she shouted. And Katie called, "What did you say?" just to make sure, because for a second she was unable to believe her ears.

So presently both the Smallbones were mounted— Katie on a small brown pony, which felt round and bouncy after Tomtit.

They looked at one another and grinned, and then Katie said, "Thank you Judy. It's ever so nice of you."

Judy was small and neat; she had a fringe, and her face made one think of a doll; her cheeks were very pink, her eyes very blue, and her teeth small and even.

"I know what it's like to have to borrow ponies. I've only had Curfew since Christmas," she answered. "He's good at bending. Just hang on to his mane if you feel unsteady; he'll do the rest. That's what I do, anyway."

Mick was lining up alongside three other ponies. He leaned forward like a jockey. "Ready, steady, go," called Miss Potter. The other children trotted. Mick won easily by at least three lengths.

He rode towards Katie, his face triumphant.

"You see, David was right," he said.

"You don't mean David Smith?" someone asked.

"Yes, that's right," cried Mick, "David Smith from the Littleheath Stables."

"You mean you know him? You are lucky."

"He's ever so nice," Katie said. "We've known him some time. Haven't we, Mick?"

"That's right."

Mick thought he read envy in the other children's faces. And Katie thought, they don't know him. And suddenly neither of them cared about their unsuitable clothes, nor about being bareback.

After that nothing could go wrong. Tomtit seemed to perform better each time he raced; Katie found Curfew easy to ride; and she couldn't help thinking, this is the first time we've ever ridden together. And it seemed that they had started something which would go on. We'll come again, she kept thinking, often. Why shouldn't we? She didn't want fame, particularly, nor admiration; but she wanted friends; to know girls like Judy; girls of her own age who rode too.

An hour later, walking and riding home, Mick said, "Glad we came? I am."

"Yes, and she said we should come again, any time we like."

"I know. But I still wish we had a saddle. Tomtit could have beaten the lot of them if only I'd had a saddle," Mick said.

"Never mind."

"But I do mind. Don't you want us to win at the Local Show?"

"Of course."

"Well then, we need a saddle."

"That's why we're riding in the gymkhana—to win some money for a saddle," Katie answered.

"If only we could borrow one. If only Paula hadn't been sent away . . ."

But Katie wasn't listening. she was thinking about the other children—how nice they were, not stuck up at all, she thought. "When I'm a girl groom, I shall work with people like that," she decided, for she knew suddenly for certain that she was going to get a job with horses when she left school.

She saw herself grooming tall thoroughbreds, plaiting manes, travelling in horse-boxes; the life seemed to hold all she had ever wanted—horses, riding, excitement, travel, friends. "So it won't matter if I fail the eleven-plus," she thought, because you don't need a grammar school education to be a girl groom.

All her problems seemed solved as they travelled homewards through the hot afternoon. Tomtit was tired, so after a time they both walked. Presently they fell to discussing the Show.

"We must get the schedule," Mick said.

"Why?"

"For the entry form, of course, you twit. And we have to pay to enter," Mick continued. "Have you got any money in your money box?"

"One pound."

"That won't be enough."

"How much have you?"

"Fifty pence."

"We'll have to ask Mum, then."

"Or Dad."

"How much do you think we'll need?"

"Not less than three pounds: probably five pounds," Mick said. They started to think about money, and suddenly the day was less lovely, just a hot, sticky, summer day. Mick began to kill flies, which swarmed round Tomtit; he killed them viciously, as though he was killing his own need for money.

"Oh dear. It's always something, really it is," complained Katie.

"Yes, always," answered Mick.

They realised now that they were hungry; the day became unbearably hot; people passed them in open cars, in sun-hats and dark glasses; with picnic baskets strapped to luggage racks.

Then at last they reached the last stretch of familiar road, passed the local pub, Tomtit pricked his ears.

"We'll give him a huge feed of oats. He deserves it," said Mick.

They couldn't help feeling despondent. Five pounds is an awful lot of money, Katie thought.

"Why does one always have to ask for things? Why does everything cost money?" wondered Mick.

They watered Tomtit, turned him out in the paddock with a bucket half full of crushed oats. We're only gloomy because we're hungry, thought Mick.

Mr Stone was drinking tea with their parents when they reached the house.

"Your dinner is in the oven," Mrs Smallbone told them. She was adding up figures. They felt unwanted as they took their lunch of lasagne from the oven.

"Yes; the cucumbers are ready," Mr Smallbone was telling Mr Stone, who sat heavily, his shoulders sagging, in the only comfortable chair in the kitchen.

"Well, how is the pony going?" asked Mr Stone, searching his pockets for tobacco.

"Very well, thank you," Mick answered.

One of the twins was crying upstairs.

"I'm glad to see him being used," Mr Stone said.

He lit his pipe. And that's something, Mick thought, he might have come to stop us riding Tomtit.

"Well, that's it, then," said Mr Stone, heaving himself out of the chair. Mick found him his stick. Mrs Smallbone had gone upstairs to the twins. "I'll be round next Saturday, then. I think you're doing very well, Bill."

He shook Mr Smallbone's hand. The kitchen smelt of tobacco. The children watched the old man go. Mrs Smallbone came downstairs.

"A girl called," she said, and for an instant Mick's heart leapt and he thought, Paula! But a second later he knew it was impossible. "She brought you this. Miss Potter said you should have it today; otherwise you'll be too late to enter or something. She came in a lovely car. She said: Just say it was Judy. They'll know."

Mick realised that his mother was impressed. He was too. He thought, we've got friends now, real friends.

Katie took the Schedule. She found the entry form, the events. "It's a pound to enter for each gymkhana event, and double that after Monday," she said. She saw now that it was hopeless; they needed five pounds just as Mick had thought; and how could they ask for five pounds? Just for themselves, for their own ends?

"Here, let me look," said Mr Smallbone, reaching for the schedule.

Mick sat thinking, if Paula was here, she would lend us the money; she's that sort of person; she would give you the coat off her back, as the saying goes.

"What is it you want to enter for?" asked Mr Smallbone. "Come on. Speak up."

The children stared at their father and then at the schedule. "Musical Chairs under fourteen, Bending under fourteen, Potato Race, Flag Race and Sack Race."

"That's five pounds," said Mr Smallbone pulling a five pound note from his pocket. "Here give me a pen, let's fill it up."

Mr Smallbone filled up the entry form, pinned the note to it, found an envelope and addressed it.

"Is there a stamp anywhere?" he asked, looking in the strange assortment of pots and jars which stood on the mantelpiece.

The children didn't know what to say. They were surprised. Mick felt as though anything could happen now. Katie went across the room and kissed her father, which was something she hadn't done for ages, because he was generally still working in the garden when she went to bed.

Chapter Twelve

PRODUCE STALL

"I believe Dad likes us riding," Katie said afterwards, when they were going to bed.

"I think so too," agreed Mick, who couldn't stop whistling now that the Show was paid for, everything was settled, the future worked out like a flagged map with the biggest flag of all on the first Sunday in August.

The following days were wet, and so was the following Saturday, which meant that they couldn't go to the White Horse Riding School. But even that didn't dampen Mick's and Katie's high spirits. They took the vegetables to the shop instead, and all the way Mick was whistling, and Tomtit seemed to catch their mood, for he trotted cheerfully, his ears pricked, his harness jingling.

"And we break up next week," exclaimed Katie, as though continuing a previous conversation.

"On Friday; and on the Sunday it's the Show," Mick replied.

"Are we going to plait Tomtit's mane?"

"Do you think you can?"

"I don't see why not. I can sew."

"The Show's just five miles away; just beyond the Riding School," Mick said. He could see them arriving, the parked horse boxes, the horsy talk all around them, checked sheets being peeled off round quarters, the judges on their shooting sticks.

I'm happier than I've ever been before, he thought suddenly. I think I did all right in the eleven-plus; I wish Paula was coming to the Show with us. She probably taught Tomtit to bend in the first place, before we had anything to do with him. But one never has everything, he thought philosophically, and now we've got far more than we've ever had before. Mum says she likes the country now, in spite of the mud and having to walk so far to post a letter. And Mick started to whistle again until Katie cried in desperation, "Oh Mick, stop!"

"Stop what."

"Whistling; it gets on my nerves. Let's talk about the Show. Did Dad enter Tomtit as Nobby or Tomtit?"

"I don't know."

Time seemed to fly after that. Days passed in a flash. The twins were talking now, and their hands were in everything—tins of golden syrup, pots of paint, the chicken's food, Tomtit's oats. The garden was full of flowers. The Beauty of Bath apples were ripe. Everything seemed to speak of prosperity and success. Katie and Mick were happy; it seemed to them now that they only lacked a saddle, and they hoped to win money towards it at the Show.

On Saturday night they groomed Tomtit for an hour. They had taken him to the blacksmith on Friday, and his feet were neat and round and well-shod. Katie had found suitable thread and needles for plaiting his mane in her mother's work-basket. The evening was red, promising a fine tomorrow.

"We've still got to clean our shoes," Katie said.

"And polish up his bridle."

"And put everything ready for the morning."

They left Tomtit munching oats, and walked slowly home without talking, each in their private world of dreams.

They found Mr Stone in the kitchen, smoking his pipe, sitting in the armchair. It was six o'clock; their mother was upstairs bathing the twins; tea was still on the table.

"Well, it seems the only thing we can do," said Mr Smallbone.

The children washed their hands.

"What's he here for?" muttered Katie.

"Ssh!" hissed Mick.

They both felt uneasy, though they couldn't have said why. A shadow seemed to be hanging over their happiness. The whole kitchen smelt how of Mr Stone's tobacco.

"Well, no-one likes working on Sunday. Not that I took much notice of Sundays when I was fit," said Mr Stone, getting out of the chair with difficulty.

Mick and Katie exchanged glances. Dad won't be able to come to the Show then, Mick thought.

They watched Mr Stone go, and evening seemed to have come rather suddenly to the little kitchen, which recently had seemed such a happy place. The children knew now that something was wrong.

Their father was about to speak, but first he was

considering which words to use, which was a bad sign.

Katie's hands felt sticky; she wiped them with her handkerchief and waited in an agony of suspense.

We can't go to the Show; that's what it is, thought Mick, and for a moment he felt nothing but blind, senseless rage. It isn't fair, his heart cried. We've worked for it; we deserve a chance, he thought. He bit his lip and waited, and somewhere far away a cow mooed.

We think we'll have to set up a stall on the road on Sundays. Mr Stone's got permission.

They couldn't blame him. They knew what their father meant; Tomtit would have to take the vegetables to the stall; he'd have to take the table too. And we'll have to drive him, Mick thought.

If only it could be any other day, thought Katie.

"But you'll still get to the Show. We're going to set it up on the main road and that's halfway there. You'll be all right kids. You're not going to miss a thing. . . ."

But he'll be tired, thought Mick. We'll have to make two journeys. He couldn't speak; he was too angry, he could only have cried, it isn't fair.

Katie sat down at the table; she wasn't hungry, but she took a piece of bread and butter because she wanted to do something.

"So you'll be all right. You're not going to miss a thing," Mr Smallbone repeated.

They tried to believe him.

"Who's going to look after the stall?" Katie asked.

"What time do your classes start?"

"Eleven o'clock in the second ring. It's Bending first, and Tomtit's best at that, isn't he, Katie?" said Mick and his voice didn't sound like his own. He had to turn away because he was afraid he'd cry.

"Yes, he's good at it, really he is."

"We'll make an early start. You can dump everything and drive on. I was hoping they'd be later than that," said Mr Smallbone. He went out into the evening to look at the sun, which had turned everything red and gold.

"I feel like committing suicide," cried Mick.

"That's wicked. What would Mum say?" asked Katie, and Mick saw that she was crying hopelessly, her tears falling in a steady stream on to the piece of bread and butter she had on her plate.

He got up, went to the window, stared at the sunset, while he tried to get his rebellious feelings under control.

His mother came downstairs, put her arms round Katie, said, "Don't cry Katie. Don't carry on so. You'll get there in time."

"But he'll be so tired. You don't understand. He'll have done miles and miles before we even get to the Show. And other ponies go in trailers and horse boxes. They don't even walk a mile," wailed Katie.

It's just our luck, thought Mick, still staring at the sunset. Have we ever had much luck? Nothing seemed possible now. It was as though the Show had been the test-case. Fate's against us, he thought, if there's such a thing as Fate.

Pride comes before a fall, though Katie, drying her eyes. We thought we had achieved so much. But I don't think we'll ever get a saddle now, not as long as we live.

"That's better," said Mrs Smallbone. "You're tired, that's the trouble. Now come on, cheer up; eat some tea. Everything will look different then."

Everything seemed even worse next morning. Climbing out of bed at six o'clock, Mick thought, first there was Paula wanting Tomtit; then when we were friends she was sent away; since then we've had to struggle on our own, except for David Smith coming once and that one morning at the Riding School. We've been looking forward to today for ages, like a drowning man clutching a straw; and now it's hopeless, the straw won't be any use. Tomtit will be too tired to bend well, too tired for anything. He banged on Katie's door before going downstairs.

"It's morning, Sunday morning," he shouted. And waking, Katie thought, what's wrong? before she remembered.

She found her brother cutting thick wedges of bread and butter in the kitchen. "Here have one," he said.

Cocks were crowing, birds were still twittering sleepily in trees when they went outside. Katie couldn't help thinking it might have been different. "I'll plait his mane, anyway," she said.

"The harness is dirty. I wish Dad had painted the cart," Mick said, and knew he was going to find fault with everything because he was in that sort of mood.

Tomtit was lying down when they reached the

paddock. He leapt guiltily to his feet when he saw them, like someone who has overslept.

They gave him oats and started to groom him with the dandy brush, which their father had bought when Paula had left such a long time ago—or, rather, what seemed such a long time ago.

Mick didn't whistle. He found fault all the time with everything. 'You're using the wrong hand. You should groom across yourself," he told Katie.

"Stand still, can't you?" he shouted at Tomtit. "Oh, these flies, how I hate them," he grumbled.

His mood didn't make Katie feel any better. She started to plait, and Tomtit's mane seemed to consist of nothing besides bristly, short hairs whose only aim in life was to remain upright. She didn't know how many plaits there should be, which end to begin—withers or forelock—and Tomtit kept shaking his head because of the flies, and Mick stood watching and saying nothing. When the mane was done there were nine plaits and the forelock, and she had broken one needle and lost another, and the time was eight o'clock.

"We're late," Mick cried. "Dad said we were to be ready by eight thirty."

They started to panic, and there are few things worse than panic. They rushed to the house, dragging Tomtit. Katie's legs felt suddenly weak and she thought, we really are going to be late—too late for anything at all. Reason vanished; the only thing in the world which mattered was the Bending Race at eleven o'clock.

"Breakfast," called Mrs Smallbone. "Breakfast."

"We haven't time," wailed Katie. "We're late." Sweat was running down her face as she pushed Tomtit's tail through the crupper and pulled up the girth, while Mick fetched the cart.

It was hot even now, unbearably hot—the kind of weather people had been praying for for years. The children pushed Tomtit between the shafts.

Mr Smallbone appeared round the corner of the house with a trestle table.

"You're late," he said.

One of Tomtit's plaits was coming out already. Katie wanted to replait it, but there wasn't time.

"Yes; I know," Mick answered. He was beginning not to care. His clothes clung to his body; the gravelled drive was hard and hot through his trainers. How can we possibly be riding in a show by eleven o'clock, he thought?

They filled the cart with boxes of tomatoes, with Beauty of Bath apples; and there were still the pears, the first luscious peaches and the flowers, which had to be transported with immense care.

"Put up the table; then one of you come back for the rest, Mum and the twins," Mr Smallbone said. The sleeves of his shirt were rolled up. "You know the place don't you? Fifty yards from the pub, by the pull-in space."

"Yes," Mick answered. The children climbed into the cart. "Come on, Tomtit," cried Mick. He couldn't trust himself to say more—he had imagined so much, the ride to the Show, their arrival, and it had come to this. Katie was sniffing into her handkerchief; there wasn't a cloud in the sky, nor a breeze to stir the trees, no noise besides the noise of the cart-wheels and of Tomtit's shoes on the hot tarmac.

Curtains were still drawn in houses; the village was deserted; only a coach passed them, loaded with happy holidaymakers.

"We may do it yet," Mick said at last.

"Yes, it's not nine yet," agreed Katie.

Tomtit was sweating; another plait had come out. His neck was lathered. He kept breaking into a walk; and the day grew hotter; flies rose up out of the hedges to meet them; dogs lay panting in the shade of porches; flowers wilted in back gardens.

They came to the pub, the parking space beyond. They climbed out of the cart, put up the table, unloaded the boxes.

"Who's going back?" asked Mick.

"I don't mind."

"Nor do I."

In the end they tossed. Katie won and chose to drive back to the market garden. "Don't be long," Mick said. "Bring some oats if you can."

She turned Tomtit and trotted away down the broad, straight road. There were more cars now. They seemed to pass in a steady stream; and there was a notice which read: To The Show. Mick sat down in the long, dry grass on the verge. He didn't want to think. He wanted simply to doze till Katie returned. But thoughts came crowding into his mind, and he couldn't escape them. He kept seeing Paula's face and remembering how she had sat on the railings evening after evening waiting for them. He was tormented by the thought of what he was missing at this very moment, for all too clearly he could see the Show already under way—the show ponies in No. 1 Ring, the under-twelves jumping in the other.

"I'm back," shrieked Katie when she reached the house. There was no sign of anyone; only a pile of boxes in the drive covered with purple tissue paper.

She loaded the boxes into the cart, and then her mother appeared, with the twins in clean dresses with washed faces and combed hair.

"What's the time?" asked Katie.

"Twenty past nine."

She pulled the twins into the cart, thinking, we may make it yet; at least there's a chance. She flicked Tomtit with the end of the reins.

"Your father's going to come on presently on the bike," said Mrs Smallbone. It was very hot now; and the twins wouldn't leave the flowers alone, and all the time Katie was seeing the Show, imagining competitors lining up for the Bending, the microphone calling numbers, the tension and the excitement.

"Don't drive so fast," said Mrs Smallbone. "You'll make the twins sick. Rachel, leave those flowers. Rachel . . ."

Chapter Thirteen

WE COULDN'T GO ON

Mick was waiting for them. "At last. I thought you were never coming," he shouted. He had seen a crowd of ponies go by, had called, "Are you going to the Show? What's the time?"

It had been ten o'clock and he had imagined an accident—one of the twins falling out of the cart, Tomtit stumbling, breaking his knees.

They took out the boxes. Then Mr Smallbone arrived.

"All right, kids, scram," he said.

They took off Tomtit's harness, put on David's bridle, started to run, leading the pony.

"You know the way?" called Mr Smallbone. "Straight through the town, then left."

"Yes," shouted Katie.

"We'll be in time," Mick said.

"Tomtit's been wonderful. Really he has," said Katie.

The cars were decreasing now. Obviously holiday-makers had reached their destinations by this time. The town, when they reached it, was quiet, almost deserted. They started to walk, and a church clock told them it was half past ten.

"We'll have to get our numbers," Mick said.

"I think we deserve to win," Katie answered.

She wished there was time to replait Tomtit's mane.

He looked scruffy now, dirty where he had sweated under the harness, tired and rather resentful.

They reached the main street, stopped for a brief moment to look in a saddler's window.

"It's not far now," Mick said.

The town was very quiet; there was a large notice at the traffic lights: To the Show. There wasn't a policeman in sight. Only an old lady walked down a street followed by a small brown dog.

They turned left at the traffic lights, and Mick thought, we're going to ride in the Show after all and, even if we don't win, we'll have made a beginning, and who knows, there may be someone there who had a saddle to spare which will fit Tomtit. He glanced at his sister; her small face looked exhausted and then suddenly she started and cried, "Stop. Listen. Oh Mick, someone screamed."

"They can't have," said Mick. "Come on. We'll be late." But Katie had stopped. "Someone screamed," she cried. "We can't go on."

"You're mad. Come on Katie," shouted Mick.

"Listen," she shouted back. And then he heard it too. A scream of "Help!" and then nothing.

He knew now that they couldn't go on. Compared to this, the Show was nothing.

"It's from the jeweller's shop," cried Katie. They started to run, dragging the surprised pony after them. A car drew up behind them; footsteps echoed down the street.

"Stop them!" shouted Mick.

"Police!" screamed Katie.

Two men came out of the jeweller's shop, calmly into the bright morning, and it seemed crazy to Katie that this could be happening here quite quietly, with no-one in sight besides themselves. "Take the car number. We can't fight them. I'm going for the police," Mick said.

He felt quite calm; the Show had disappeared completely from his mind. He vaulted on to Tomtit, and galloped away down the street, feeling like a good character in a Western, not like Mick Smallbone at all.

Katie was afraid alone there in the street. But the driver of the car was revving up the engine. She read the number plate, F267 BLX. She searched for something to throw, started to yell, "Help! Help! Help! Police!" before she remembered the scream and began running towards the jeweller's shop.

She had to force herself to go down the alleyway at the side, to climb through a broken window at the back. There was a smell of fireworks and Katie thought the men must have blown a safe. She wished that Mick would come back. Then she saw that a man was lying on the threshold of the shop in a pool of blood. He was quite old, and wore bedroom slippers. She stood looking at him for a moment and saw that he was still breathing. Inside the shop was havoc: The glass show-cases were broken, glass and tissue paper lay on the floor.

She started to scream again. "Help! Police!" Then she saw a telephone on the far side of the shop. A moment later she was dialling 999. Hours seemed to pass before anyone answered. She cried, "Ambulance," and turned to look at the old man, who hadn't moved. "Address, please," said someone. "I don't know it. It's a jeweller's in the main street. It's been burgled."

A moment later she put down the telephone, turned to look at the old man again, tried to remember the first aid she had learned as a Brownie two years ago.

Mick galloped recklessly. He had heard the car revving up behind him. He had looked back, read the number, seen that it was a black Sierra Estate. The street was still empty.

He wondered who had screamed, and hoped Katie was all right. He could see the show-ground now, a policeman directing traffic outside it.

He halted Tomtit, yelled, "Police! There's been a raid on the jeweller's in the main street."

Everything seemed to happen very quickly after that. Three policemen appeared at once, closely followed by a patrol car. They took down the number of the Sierra, and an inspector picked up the radio telephone in the patrol car, and started to organise road blocks while two constables were despatched to the shop. All the time Mick could hear the loudspeaker on the show-ground announcing, "Will entries for Class three, Bending, under fourteen, please go to the Collecting Ring." It seemed to come to him from another world. Overhead a plane droned and there was the same cloudless sky which had been above him all day. Yet nothing seemed the same any more. The despair of the early morning seemed to belong to another life; there was only one of Katie's plaits left in Tomtit's mane to remind him of it, nothing else at all.

"You'd better come with us, son," a burly constable told him. There were more police now; and the loudspeaker was silent, but in the distance he could hear the sound of thundering hoofs. He remembered for an instant that he should be there, racing with the others, trying to win a saddle. Instead, he was riding through the town talking to the police. An ambulance went by, its siren sounding. He could see now that there were several people outside the jeweller's shop. Tomtit felt tired; Mick had to urge him all the time with his legs; otherwise he would have stopped, have stood with his head drooping, in the middle of the street. Mick could see that stretcher-bearers were going into the jeweller's shop. He couldn't see Katie. Yet she must have called the ambulance, and that meant she was all right.

After replacing the telephone, Katie went back to the old man. She saw now that he had a livid wound on his forehead. She didn't touch him. She hadn't touched anything besides the telephone. She knelt down beside him. "There's an ambulance coming," she said. "You'll be all right soon, really you will."

She felt horribly alone—more alone, in fact, than she would have felt without the old man. She kept thinking, suppose the thieves have left something behind, and come back. She thought, I'll never forget this as long as I live. I wish Mick would come.

Then a voice cried, "Are you there, missy!" she unbolted the back door, and at the same moment heard an ambulance coming down the street. The Constable came in, asked, "Where's the body?"

"There," replied Katie pointing. "But he isn't dead."

"I'm glad to hear it." The siren had stopped. There were many voices outside now, all seeming to talk at once, and in the distance the could hear hoofs coming down the street.

"Do you think you'll catch the men?" she asked the Constable.

"Thanks to you and your brother's prompt action, I think we will," he answered.

Two stretcher-bearers came in. "Good afternoon, Constable. Can we move the case yet" the first asked? "Not yet. We want a few details first."

And Katie thought, I wish they'd help the poor man. I'm sure he should be in hospital.

More police were arriving now, and one in a peaked cap said, "Your brother's outside with the pony, Miss, if you'd like to wait with him."

Katie went out into the sunlight again, and found Mick looking small and grimy in comparison with the Constable and the ambulance men.

"It doesn't look as though we'll be in time for the Bending now," she said. She thought he would care, but he only said, 'It doesn't seem to matter now, does it? what's the man like who screamed?"

"Old. I don't think he's the jeweller. I think he just lives on the premises; perhaps he has a flat upstairs," suggested Katie.

"Where did they hit him?"

"On his head, I think."

"Do you think he'll die?"

"I don't know."

They made way for the ambulance men. The stretcher was half-covered by a blanket, but Katie saw with a rush of pleasure that the old man's eyes were open, and she thought he smiled at her.

The policeman in the peaked cap followed. "Have you time to pop round the corner to the station? It's only a minute away. We'd like a full description of the men from you both. I'm afraid you may have to appear in court at some later date," he said.

"That's all right," Mick answered. He was feeling grown-up now. No-one else at school had appeared in court to give evidence. They won't be able to laugh at our accents after this, he thought.

They gave evidence in turn, while the other one held the pony outside the red brick police station.

Afterwards the Inspector thanked them both; as they were leaving another policeman appeared and said, "We've caught your two men just outside the town. They were about to ditch the car ..." He slapped them on the shoulders and said, "Well done, kids! They still had all the goods with them."

Katie wanted to ask about the old man, whether he was only a tenant on the premises and whether he would recover. But Mick was already walking away along the street, leading the tired bay pony.

"There's no point in going to the Show now. Look at the time," he cried, staring at a clock. "The Bending's over, and probably the Musical Poles too. Anyway, Tomtit's tired. Look at him . . ." He felt flat now, deflated. We won't get a saddle now, he thought. "And we might have met Paula there. But how can we go now? We look in such a mess." And it was true. Tomtit's sweat had dried in a thick crust; the children's faces were hot and dusty, Katie's clothes were filthy and cobwebbed from climbing through the back window; and they were tired. So much had happened so quickly. There had been the panic in the morning, all the rushing about, the return of hope, then the climax of the scream. And this is the anticlimax, thought Mick as they walked back through the hot, empty town.

They could hear the twins crying long before they reached the stall.

"Hello there. How did it go?" called Mr Smallbone, and they saw that half the fruit and flowers and vegetables had gone. "You're back soon."

"We didn't get to the Show. There was a robbery in the town. We got mixed up with it," Mick said.

"At the jeweller's. An old man got knocked down. We heard him scream. We couldn't go on after that," explained Katie.

Mick was regretting not going to the Show now. He looked at Tomtit and knew that he wouldn't have won, anyway, because the pony was tired even before they reached the town.

He thought, we did the right thing. But why must life be so difficult? Why couldn't we have simply gone to the Show as we planned in the beginning? Standing there telling his parents what had happened, he was suddenly sure of nothing. What obstacles might appear to stop him being a vet? Why should he succeed?

At the moment they only wanted one thing—a saddle. Yet everyone conspired to stop them having it.

Katie was drying the twins' eyes. Perhaps one isn't meant to have everything. Perhaps it means we'll have more in the next world, she thought. But it didn't console her; she almost wished that they hadn't stopped, that they had gone on to the Show. All that practising for nothing. And we told all the kids at school that we'd be there. They'll think we funked it, she thought.

"So that's my five pounds gone west," said Mr Smallbone. "But I'm glad you helped the police. You did the right thing there."

They let Tomtit graze the verge . . . Mrs Smallbone produced lunch from a hamper—home-made veal and ham pie, crisps, bananas, oranges and lemonade.

"I suppose there'll be other shows," said Mr Smallbone. "I think you were wrong to turn back, though. You wouldn't have won in any case, now would you? But you would have gained some experience, if you see what I mean."

"Tomtit was tired," said Mick stubbornly.

"We've made thirty pounds," said Mr Smallbone, loading the boxes into the cart.

Tomtit scowled at his harness when Mick started to put it on. He was besieged by flies. Katie had taken the remaining plait out, and his mane stood upright, as though he was in Norway. "Home, John and don't spare the horses," cried Mr Smallbone, and Mick and Katie could see that he at any rate was happy. As they started homewards along the main road, the first riders to leave the Show clattered past them, rosettes pinned to their ponies' bridles.

Chapter Fourteen

THE SADDLE

They didn't practise gymkhana events any more. Instead, they concentrated on the pigs and chickens, and delivered vegetables in the cart. But they still longed for a saddle; the longing was there at the backs of their minds whenever they looked at Tomtit, when they wakened in the morning, when they went to bed at night. Their parents knew how they felt and kept promising.

"Next year. Next summer, when we've got through our first winter, we'll buy a saddle," they promised; and to Mick and Katie next summer seemed years and years away. They saved their pocket money; they bought raffle tickets.

"If only the robbery hadn't happened," said Katie again and again. "If we had ridden bareback at the Show, someone would have noticed us, would have taken pity on us, would have lent us a saddle."

"And if it hadn't fitted we could have bought a numnah later on," Mick said.

Three days passed.

On the fourth day, when they were feeding the pigs after tea, they heard hoofs coming along the road. They stopped and stared over the hedge as they always did when they heard hoofs, and a voice called, "Hello."

"It's Paula! She's come back," cried Mick.

He threw down the pig bucket. "Hello. When did you get home?" he cried. He could see now that she was riding a short-backed black pony with two white socks and a star. She was wearing an open-necked blue shirt and jodhpurs. She hadn't changed. She looked just the same as she did when they first met in March.

"This is Midnight. Do you like him? My new school is brilliant. One does more or less what one likes, with the result that one works much harder. At least, I did, and Midnight's my reward," Paula explained.

Katie couldn't take her eyes off the saddle; it was the one she had ridden on, which she had always considered Tomtit's.

"He's very nice; so well put together," Mick answered, hoping he sounded professional. "I like his eyes as well. You are lucky."

"I had to work for him. I really swotted. You can have Tomtit to yourselves now without me butting in. Won't that be a relief? We can ride together if you want to."

"That will be marvellous," cried Mick. "Really smashing."

"How's Sinbad?" asked Katie at last, fighting back envy.

"Oh fine. Just the same. He hasn't changed. I suppose I'd better go now. I don't want to be in trouble again," Paula said. "By the way, I suppose you've got a saddle by this time. You must have. Only Midnight goes so fast, you'd never keep up without a saddle."

Mick didn't want to give a straight answer, because at that moment he wanted to ride with Paula more than almost anything else in the world. But Katie was looking straight at him, daring him to tell the truth with her eyes.

"Not yet, but we soon will," he answered.

"Well, hurry up, because I'm not going to ride with you until you have one—it's far too nerve-racking and I loathe accidents," said Paula, starting to ride away on Midnight.

They said nothing to one another, and stood watching Paula guide her pony on to the verge at the side of the road. They watched her give him the aid to canter. They could see that he was a well-schooled pony, that he moved beautifully, that he and Paula were a good combination.

"We'd better finish feeding the pigs," said Mick at last. He didn't want to discuss their predicament, but Katie cried, "It's much better to give up trying— to stop hoping, isn't it? We only get one disappointment after another."

"The answer is, count your blessings, I suppose. After all, we've got the use of all our limbs," Mick said.

"I never did like Paula," Katie said. "Or not really deep down. And I like her even less today."

Mick didn't answer. The pigs were squealing; until they were fed, the children couldn't hear their mother calling, "Mick, Katie, there's a gentleman to see you. Mick, Katie . . ."

"Perhaps it's David," suggested Katie.

They didn't hurry. The sun was setting. Somewhere sheep were bleating and there was the ageless peace of a summer evening hanging over everything.

There was a Rolls Royce parked by the notice which read Hillsborough Market Garden, by the blackboard below which read: Lettuces 30p each, Radishes 40p a bunch, Spring Onions 50p a bunch, Beauty of Bath Apples 30p a lb, Cut Flowers.

"That's a beautiful car," Mick said. He was still feeling limp. He had been pleased to see Paula; but her remark about the saddle had dashed all his hopes.

Their mother met them on the path. "He's called Mr Castle. He wants to talk to you about the robbery. Perhaps he's going to give you a reward," she said. But even that didn't raise their spirits, because they had given up hoping for things.

Mr Castle was standing in the front room looking out of the window.

"Mick and Katie?" he said when they entered, and held out his hand, and they were suddenly embarrassed because they hadn't washed the pig food off their hands.

He said, "It doesn't matter. There's no need to shake hands, is there?" And they saw that he was tall, with a high forehead and receding hair, that he wore a suit and suede shoes.

"Won't you sit down, sir?" Mick said.

He said, "I've come to thank you. You've saved my firm a great deal of trouble and a great deal of expense. We have a chain of jewellery shops, and the one which was robbed last Sunday was one of ours. Does that ring a bell?"

"It certainly does, sir," Mick answered.

"Really it does," echoed Katie.

Mum's right. He is going to give us a reward, the children thought.

"And you missed going to the Show because of it. My daughters ride, so I know how much that meant to you . . ." Mr Castle continued. "You've got the use of a pony, I understand, but no saddle, your mother tells me. Now, I have a suggestion to make. How about my firm getting a saddle made for your pony by the local saddler?"

Mick and Katie stared at him. It seemed unbelievable. It was as though money had suddenly started to grow on the trees outside. At last they were going to have a saddle.

"Oh thank you," cried Mick.

We'll be able to ride with Paula now, Katie thought. To go to the rallies like other children. No-one need be sorry for us ever again.

"But I haven't finished," Mr Castle continued, watching the children's faces. "A saddle isn't much of a reward considering you saved us more than £10,000 in jewellery and cash. I want you to get fitted out in riding clothes too, at the firm's expense. I'll let you have a letter to that effect. And I want you to have riding lessons. Is there a good riding school near here? I suggest a course of twenty four for each of you."

For a moment Mick and Katie couldn't speak. This is really happening, Mick thought. We're going to have lessons and a saddle.

"The White Horse Stables, Miss Potter's," he said.

"Let me write it down. And the name of the big shop in the town, I can't remember its name. I know—I'll get the saddler to send a man to measure the pony for a saddle and bridle. How's that?"

"Fantastic. It's amazing," Mick cried.

Mr Castle sat writing, while Mick and Katie stood seeing the future, which had somersaulted so swiftly from hopelessness to hopefulness, and which now stretched before them full of friends and equitation, of sunlit rides, of new clothes and new tack.

"And finally," continued Mr Castle, putting away his notebook, "I have only to add this. I think you're extremely brave youngsters. I think you're a credit to the country, and later on, when Miss Potter thinks you're fit, I hope you'll have my youngest daughter's pony, which will be looking for a home this year or next. She's a mare of fourteen one."

It's like a book, thought Katie. A film or something, she kept thinking, it can't be happening to us. But Mr Castle was there before them, tall, elegant and kind.

They said, "Thank you. Thank you so much for everything."

"I can't stop. I just dropped in because I was passing. But I'll let you have everything in writing, so you'll have my address. Goodbye, and again thank you. I'm afraid you may have to appear in court, but you won't mind that, will you?"

"No. Thank you. Thank you so much." Mr Castle let himself out, strode away down the path, while Mick and Katie stared at one another, and now the evening seemed full of sunlight, the future lit by unquenchable hope. "We'll each have a pony to ride, then . . ." Katie said.

"Twenty four riding lessons. Isn't it wonderful? Mum, have you heard?" cried Mick.

"Dad," cried Katie. "We're going to be given a saddle and later on a pony."

They ran out of the front room. They felt suddenly capable of anything; of jumping at the biggest shows in England one day, of winning point-to-points, and of hunting. They seemed to have everything they had ever wanted. "And it's all because we stopped when we heard that scream. After all, we might have gone on," Mick said.

"Mum says the old man's all right, and that we're mentioned in the paper just a little bit," Katie said.

"What's happened?" asked Mr Smallbone. "Has Christmas come or something?"

"Oh, it's wonderful, Dad," cried Katie. "We're going to have everything we ever wanted, everything. I can't believe it . . ."

"But even when we get the other pony, we must still love Tomtit," mused Mick.

They gazed round the kitchen as though they were drunk; and then Mick started to whistle, on and on, as though he would never stop.

"Well, I must say you deserve it. You deserve every bit of it," said Mrs Smallbone, and Katie saw suddenly that there were tears in her mother's eyes. "Oh Mum, don't cry," she cried.

"I can't help it, I'm so happy."

"I think this calls for a cup of tea," said Mrs Smallbone.

"And later on we'll be able to teach the twins to ride—properly, because we will have had lessons," Mick said, and he saw himself standing in the middle of the paddock, as Paula had, calling, "Toes up. Shorten your reins. Very good. Well done," And there seemed no limit to his happiness.

"And we'll never miss anything for want of a saddle. Not as long as we live," cried Katie. And she began to laugh, to dance round the table and sing, as no-one had ever seen her do before. And slowly twilight came, unnoticed by the Smallbones. For Mick was seeing the past stretching behind him, a long, rough road with a steep hill at the end. And now they had reached the summit and before them lay everything they had dreamed about so often.

Katie simply went on dancing and singing, "For want of a saddle the rallies were lost. For want of a saddle the hunts were lost. For want of a saddle the races were doomed. Oh, I'm so happy, really I am."

Two weeks later to the day, Katie and Mick stood staring at their saddle. The saddler had been obliging.

"I'll make it a rush-job for you." forward-cut, deep-seated, with knee-rolls, it was the small cross-country saddle they had asked for after telephoning David for advice. They stared at it for a time and then they went upstairs and dressed in skull-caps, jodhpurs, shirts, ties and hacking jackets, and suddenly they looked exactly like the children who rode at Miss Potter's. They stared at one another. They started to laugh, to sing. "Now we'll go and surprise Paula!" cried Mick. "She won't recognise us."

126

"And tomorrow we start our riding lessons," Katie said.

"And become great riders—so good that we'll have Mr Castle's daughter's pony this autumn, in time for the hunting season," cried Mick. "Dad says we can. He says the garden's doing fine.

"Skull-caps do suit us," cried Katie, looking at her brother. "You look like a jockey."

"And you look like a show rider," Mick said.

They ran downstairs, out into the sunlight. "We're going to ride," they shouted to their mother. Mick picked up the saddle, Katie the egg-butt snaffle and, looking as fashionable as ever, their heads in the clouds, they hurried through the walled garden, opened the gate into the drive, started to run again, Mick singing at the top of his voice and Katie thinking, what will Paula say? We'll be able to do everything now, just like other horsy children. Seeing them, Tomtit raised his head and whinnied, and to them at that moment he was the most beautiful pony in the world.